*Searching for Alice*

Peter Arnds

# SEARCHING FOR ALICE

### A Novel

**DALKEY ARCHIVE PRESS**

Library of Congress Cataloging-in-Publication Data

Names: Arnds, Peter O., 1963- author.
Title: Searching for Alice / Peter Arnds.
Description: First Dalkey Archive edition. | McLean, IL : Dalkey Archive
Press, 2018.
Identifiers: LCCN 2018027178 | ISBN 9781628973143 (paperback : alk. paper)
Subjects: | GSAFD: Bildungsromans.
Classification: LCC PR6051.R615 S43 2018 | DDC 823/.914--dc23
LC record available at https://lccn.loc.gov/2018027178


www.dalkeyarchive.com
McLean, IL / Dublin

Printed on permanent/durable acid-free paper.

# PROLOGUE

*WHEN HE SAW his canoe sink and his shoes drift downriver he had only one thought: how am I going to walk out of here? Some of his things, however, had got caught by the very branches that had caused his boat to capsize. His rifle stuck out from an entanglement of twigs, and he was able to salvage the two tin cans, one containing the powder and the lead, the other his papers. The bowie knife too had not been lost, he kept it strapped to his belt at all times. He took hold of the cans, the frying pan, and his gun, and raising everything above his head swam the short distance to shore.*

*A kookaburra sat on the branch right above him, laughing at him. Here he was, hundreds of miles from anywhere. Everyone had warned him against the trip in the first place. He had been an experienced backwoodsman in Arkansas, but this was the Australian bush. Nobody had ever attempted to paddle down the entire length of this river. It was a foolish idea, people had told him in Sydney and on the coach that took him to Albury. There had been a sixteen-month drought, and besides, he would find hostile native tribes along many stretches of the river, which had so many curves that what seemed like a six-hundred-mile voyage was in fact more than a thousand miles. It was impossible, they had said, and easy to make mistakes, mistakes that could cost him his life.*

*Of course, the mistake was that instead of keeping his boots tied to his feet he had taken them off and placed them next to him so that he could just step out of the boat whenever the snags made it impossible to continue or when the river was too shallow. Next time he'd know. If there ever was to be a next time. God only knew how many miles he was from the nearest sheep station. This trip, he thought, was getting rather interesting. Generally he was fond of dangerous situations, they added spice to his travels, but how was he going to walk any extensive distance without shoes in terrain that made his feet bleed after half an hour? For a moment, he thought of the bunyip again, but he doubted it had been the cause of the accident.*

# CHAPTER 1
## *VERGANGENHEITSBEWÄLTIGUNG*

"WHAT ARE YOU reading there?"

He slipped the Gerstäcker book into his schoolbag: "Sorry. I had to look something up. It won't happen again." Lowering his head he checked whether he had copied it right—all those humungous German words—capital V, one umlaut, twenty-five letters. All German words ending in –ung are feminine. Otherwise, grammatical gender follows no apparent logic. The moon is masculine, carrots feminine, girls neute—*der Mond, die Karotte, das Mädchen.*

Suddenly the door opened. Frau Grummler turned from the blackboard and put the chalk down. Sometimes she could not control herself and threw things at students, the chalk or the exam books. Those she threw like a Frisbee, or like the hat with the metal edge the Chinese guy throws in the James Bond movie.

A new girl had walked in, her head reaching the top frame of the door. The classroom fell silent.

"This is Alice Rubinstein," said Frau Grummler. "Our exchange student from Australia. She will be with us through the end of the year. Why don't you sit over there, Alice?"

She sat down right next to him.

"*Vergangenheitsbewältigung*," Frau Grummler resumed. "Make sure you spell it right! Don't forget the umlaut. Don't think of *Welt.* It has more to do with *Gewalt.* Violence, Alice. You do know German, don't you?"

Alice nodded. "My mother is . . . well, *was* German. But I don't know that word."

Her accent was slight.

3

"That's fine," said Frau Grummler. "I think in English you'd say something like 'mastering' or 'controlling the past.'"

"How do you do that?"

The question had just popped out of him, almost uncontrollably. Grummler seemed surprised, too, for he was usually not the one to ask questions.

"How do you do what, Jonathan?"

"How do you master the past?"

She paused, then said something about how it wasn't healthy to hold anything in for a long time, followed by a quick mention of Freud.

What an odd name, he thought—*Freud, Freude.* Joy.

Alice kept stretching her legs. They stuck out a good bit on the other side of the desk. She sat so close to him that he could smell her. It was an intriguing smell, and he was sure he had encountered it before, there was a distant memory of it, he just didn't have an image in his head.

Frau Grummler put in that awful videotape again. They had been watching it day after day, in German class, in History, even Religion. He was fifteen and had never seen mass shootings, all those bloodied white bodies slung into each other and heaped up in the ditches, some of them still moaning so they had to be shot again. It all happened not so long ago, maybe thirty-five years earlier.

They sat through another half hour of it. "We'll survive," says Frau Weiss, the Jewish doctor's wife. "This is the country of Beethoven, Schiller, and Mozart." Her husband is skeptical. He says: "'Unfortunately, none of them are in office right now." Just having lost their home, mother and daughter sit down at the Bechstein piano one last time. They are singing the Loreley, Heine's famous woman by the Rhine, who pulls boatmen who stare at her deep into the river: *Ich weiss nicht, was soll es bedeuten, dass ich so traurig bin.* "She cast a spell that enchants me, and no happiness can I find. For she is a legend that haunts me," etc.

"Why do you think the song was forbidden," asked Grummler.

Nobody had an answer.

"And what happened to Anna Weiss, their young daughter? Why has she become so unresponsive after her encounter with the German soldiers?"

"She was raped," said Alice, in English.

"Yes," said Grummler, "correct. And in German: *vergewaltigen. Sie wird vergewaltigt.*"

The class was quiet. Everyone figured out what happened to her afterwards in the Hadamer sanatorium where under the disguise of therapy the mentally ill were murdered. "Euthanasia," said Grummler, "it's Greek for beautiful death, *eu* means beautiful, *thanatos* death."

He looked at Alice. She just stared at the teacher. Was she shellshocked? Wondering what kind of a sick place she'd arrived in?

During recess he walked over to her. Even leaning against the fence, her hips at an angle, she was taller than all the others.

"Do they make you watch films like that in Australia?"

His heart was beating fast. Had she understood him? Should he repeat himself? It had taken him a while to string these words together. English still didn't come naturally to him; it didn't rise from the belly the same way German did; he had to think about each sentence, translate word for word. He was always happy, though, for an opportunity to speak it. English was a refuge for him, a door to somewhere better.

"Not really," she said, looking at him.

They quickly became friends. When he looked at Alice, he pictured her in that wild sunny place on the other side of the planet, saw himself with her, walking along a deserted beach; he had seen many pictures of it, had often mentally transported himself there, swimming in crystal-clear turquoise water under endless blue skies. He could feel the heat on his skin as he stared out the classroom window, at the gray stubble fields under a brooding North German winter sky.

"What's there to do around here?" she asked him one day.

"Not much. This place isn't as exciting as Australia."

"That depends. It's not that exciting where I'm from. It's small. You have to drive for thousands of kilometers to get anywhere else. There's beautiful scenery nearby though. The area is full of red hills, ghost gums, and billabongs."

"What are ghost gums and billabongs?"

"White eucalyptus trees and water holes."

He could feel the Australian landscape inside him.

"We don't have water holes," he said, "but if you like trees, I'll show you my favorite."

That day he took her up to the *Kurpark*, past its small Renaissance palace and the seven fossilized footprints of a Tyrannosaurus Rex who'd once passed through the area. Now the place was populated mostly by older people on their way to clinics and the thermal pools. This was a German spa town, one among hundreds scattered all over the country, places full of rheumatism, skin disorders, heart and stomach failure, elevated blood pressure, and circulation weaknesses. *Kreislaufschwäche*, they called it, a word that sounded to him like a death sentence, although it really just meant having cold feet. It's a popular diagnosis, his father once said, enabling even younger people to take six weeks off from work so they could visit this place and drink water smelling of rotten eggs, or submerge their bodies in heavy mud baths. For the most part, however, they were pensioners. They still remembered all the bad years he was now learning about, and they had a hearty dislike for children—kids who would sometimes yell with the ecstasy of a childhood yet unbroken.

"Where are we going?" she asked.

"To the *Buchenwald*."

She was frowning.

"Wasn't that a concentration camp?"

"Yes. But it's nothing like that."

Deeper and deeper into the park they went, where nature was less controlled, and past huge boulders rounded by the last ice age. There was a small forest here, a *Wald*, which consisted entirely of beech trees.

"*Buchen*," he said, pointing at the Wald. "This is our Buchenwald."

"Then why was the concentration camp called Buchenwald?"

"Because they didn't want to just call it a concentration camp."

"You mean they gave it a better name so that people wouldn't suspect what was going on?"

"Yes, something like that. The Nazis were fond of giving nice names to evil things."

"It's a euphemism," she said.

"Right. Like what Grummler told us about euthanasia, the beautiful death. It was just mass murder."

The trees up here were growing every which way.

"There it is."

"What?"

"*Mein Lieblingsbaum.* My favorite tree."

It was bent over in a high arch across the path, just like a bridge, with its roots partially exposed and its crown touching the ground again on the other side. Although uprooted, the tree was alive, and every spring it budded with bright green leaves.

The top of the arch was another refuge from the world at large. Climbing up and getting across and down the other side wasn't too difficult if you sat on the broad trunk and moved your legs forward slowly, all the way up the curve of the bridge. It must have been at least twelve feet off the ground.

"It's beautiful!" she said. "Like something from a fairy tale."

She was standing next to the labyrinth of unearthed roots. They looked like the wild Medusa hair around her head. She climbed up and over with great ease, and when she stood next to him again he noticed how red her cheeks were with the freshness of spring.

It became their secret getaway spot. They met there after school and sat next to each other at the top of the bridge, looking out over the fields and hills to the south.

"Those hills over there," she said one day. "They're full of mineshafts, right?"

He was surprised she knew this. Papa had often spoken of them, how some of them ran the length of the hills and surfaced again on the other side, while other passages never found an exit.

"How do you know about the mines?"

"Mom used to tell me."

"How does *she* know?"

"She's from around here. When I was a kid she used to tell us that the Pied Piper led the children of Hamelin into one of those mines. They had to walk all the way through the center of the earth until they came out again on the other side in Central Australia."

"How weird! Why would the Pied Piper take the kids from Hamelin to Australia?"

"They needed people there. To settle."

She laughed.

"What is it?"

"It's funny but it's almost like my mother's one of those children following the Piper. She came from here and settled in the middle of Australia."

A noise made her turn.

Two boys stood almost right underneath them. One of them was Manfred, the son of the *Schlachtermeister*, the butcher.

"Hey, *ihr da oben*," it came yelling from beneath. "Don't you know this is our territory?"

Manfred was the strongest boy at school. The reason, it was rumored, for his unusual strength was the pigs' blood he had been raised on. Every morning on his way to school Jonathan would pass by the butcher's shop window where Manfred's father hung up strings of fresh sausages like a curtain of meat. From a good distance Jonathan could already hear the pigs squeal. Their smell, the smell of swine in agony, would get stronger with every step. Sometimes, he would even catch a glimpse of Manfred's father driving a gigantic knife into pink flesh.

A stick came flying.

"Come off that tree!"

Alice looked at the boy, then at him, so he climbed down. But before he had even reached the ground Manfred was on him, making him stumble backwards against the roots.

"*Angsthase*! You coward!"

"What's your problem? You really wanna fight over a tree? *Sei doch nicht blöd!*"

"You calling me stupid?"

The punch that hit him in the middle of his face was like concrete and sent his glasses flying, making the world an instant blur.

"Jonathan!" Alice shrieked.

"Jonathan!" Manfred was mocking her, squeezing the vowels. "Is he your little baby?"

Jonathan was ready for the next punch, aimed straight at the face. He ducked quickly, then rammed his head into Manfred's stomach. The butcher's son bent over like a snap knife. Jonathan felt his own fist shooting forward. With utmost precision, as if guided by some invisible force, it came from below and landed on his opponent's chin.

Manfred's face was distorted in pain. He spat.

Spat again.

Stared in horror.

Not a single word came out of his bleeding mouth. Manfred looked over at his friend, then at Alice. She had jumped off the tree and picked up Jonathan's spectacles. There was no chance to get past Manfred and his friend, the only way away was up again, up the arching tree. It wasn't until he reached the highest point that they followed, closing in on him, one from each side.

Manfred was still bleeding from his mouth, his red hair sticking up like the flames of hell, and the eyes of a maniac. When they had come to within a few feet, Jonathan leaned forward and hugged the trunk, breathing in deeply the smell of its bark. Clasping it between his arms, with his hands folded in prayer, he let his legs slide. Hanging in midair he was ready to jump when he felt his knees being touched.

It was Alice.

"Come," she said. She locked her arms around his thighs the way he had hugged the tree and said: "Let go."

Her strength surprised him. She kept holding on and he let go. It was just a second or two, but the moment did not seem to end. They had become one gigantic body reaching almost all the way up to the highest point of the natural bridge.

Slowly, gently, she let him slide down until he reached the ground. "Run."


They took off as fast as they could. Jonathan had a hard time catching up with her as they ran down the hill, past the fossilized Tyrannosaurus Rex footprints, the Renaissance palace, and the spa patients turning heads in alarm at so much youthful exuberance.

It was almost dark by now.

"Do you know a good hiding place?"

Still panting, he suggested one of the many pastry shops. There was one that had a back room. It exuded the healing promise of pralines, and a mix of eau-de-Cologne and moth powder hung about the place.

They picked a table in the back corner where the light was dimmer. When the waitress finally arrived he ordered two *Baumkuchen*, a local specialty consisting of chocolate-coated sponge cake.

"Looks a bit like your tree."

It was true. It did have the shape of a perfect arch.

He also ordered some *Kurschlamm*, spa mud, the other local specialty concocted in honor of the many patients and consisting of little rocky-road-like praline heaps dipped in chocolate.

"These look a bit like scat, don't you think? Kangaroo scat."

He had never seen kangaroo scat, let alone a kangaroo, but in a way she was right, the pralines looked just like little lumps of turd, but with undigested pieces in it, almond splinters, which spiked the curves.

"Why is that guy such a bully?"

"I don't know. We never got along. And maybe—"

"Maybe what?"

"I think Manfred's got a crush on you."

His head grew hot as he said this.

"Forget him! Let's talk about something else. Anyway, thanks for showing me your favorite place around here. One day maybe I'll show you my favorite places in Australia. Lake McKenzie, for one. And another, near where I live."

"What are they like?"

"McKenzie is a blue lake in the middle of the bush. You'd love it. The other one is called Ellery Creek. It's a billabong. You can swim across it to the other side and lie on a beach between two big cliffs. The Aboriginals call it Udepata, and it's an important site on the honey-ant dreaming trail."

"The what?"

"The honey-ant dreaming. That's an Aboriginal songline."

He didn't understand, but her words had a strange effect on him. He sensed that there was a world of things to learn out there. Udepata, dreaming trail, songline—what beautiful words they were.

They didn't leave the café until it was dark.

She was digging around in her coat. "Can you pay? I must have lost my wallet by the tree."

"Do you want to go back?"

"No, it's too dark, and I should have been home ages ago. I'll go first thing in the morning."

It was chilly outside, and no stars. When they got to her place she suddenly touched his hand, pulling him closer. They hugged for a long time. He still couldn't place her smell, but again it seemed familiar somehow.

"Here. Get on the step, will you," she said suddenly.

A little hesitantly, clumsily, their lips met.

The bad thing about gravity is that it's so predictable, but kissing Alice he felt as if he'd suddenly become weightless.

Three rabbits dashed forth from a bush.

He immediately disengaged from the kiss and looked into her eyes. Had she noticed?

"See you Monday," she said, kissing him lightly on the forehead. Then she unlocked the door and was swallowed by the darkness.

Monday morning came but Alice was missing from school.

Tuesday went by. Wednesday, slowly.

He waited the entire week, watching every day for her return. The teachers refused to say why she'd left, so he went to the house where she had been staying. He looked at the name sign on the door. Rubinstein. Alice's last name.

An old man opened the door. There was something foreign about him. He looked at Jonathan suspiciously. Alice? She had to go home. Why? No answer. Where exactly was home? Had she left an address? The man was getting impatient. Look, young man, he said, she's back home. That's all there is to it.

For a long time he kept thinking about her. With his Swiss army knife he carved a heart into the bark of the arched tree, J + A inside it. And into the headboard of his bed he carved:

BURY ME IN AUSTRALIA.

*Gerstäcker, he thought, must have tempted fate just like this sometimes.*

*Coming from his long voyage across South America, where he'd walked across the Cordilleras in winter, then travelling on to Tahiti, he arrived in Australia in April 1851. Sydney in those days seemed to have little to do with romance, it was all business here, pounds and shillings being the only magic words to light up the faces of the people surrounding the stranger. His pounds quickly turned into shillings. He arrived with a bundle of preconceived ideas about the Australians, but soon realized that he would have to relinquish the idea of having been thrown into a consummate collection of murderers, thieves, housebreakers, and other desperate characters. Having expected to be robbed within an hour of his arrival, he had to admit to himself that it was just a prejudice, this place being in no way worse than others he had seen. Those who had once been convicts had long repented of their sins and graduated to the status of perfectly honorable citizens. For anyone arriving here and settling down, he writes, the past was immediately forgotten.*

*He stayed in Sydney as long as it took him to get ready for his canoe trip down the Murray. His purpose was as practical as it was idealistic: not only did he want to explore the river's navigability, he was also keen on seeing the bunyip rumored to live in its waterways and nearby billabongs.*

*Setting off one fine morning, he travelled by coach as far as Albury, where he spent a week looking for the right tree trunk to carve a canoe from. Having lived for years in the backwoods of Arkansas he was used to the pines and spruces of North America, from which it had been easy to build canoes, season them to perfection, then to shoot down the Fourche La Fave or the Buffalo River at the speed of an arrow. Part of his longing for Australia had always been to see its bush and forests, but on his journey to the Murray he became terribly disappointed. Gums—gums—gums wherever the eye sought out another growth of trees. Gums—whether they called them white or red gums, or stringy barks or iron barks or even, by way of flattery, apple trees—they were all gums, everlasting, evergreen, shedding their bark in the winter. It proved exceedingly difficult to build a canoe from one of these. The problem with the stringy barks he examined was that they were all rotten inside. As soon as he got his axe into them they would split and crumble. He finally found one that was serviceable enough and started hollowing it out, encouraged and admired by his hosts in Albury, who assured him that his cause was a noble one, for it would make the Murray more accessible to future navigation. But they warned him about the dangers of his undertaking: nobody had ever attempted such a journey, and he'd be sure to be speared to death for his kidney fat. When they saw his resolve, however, they did all they could to help him.*

*Before long, the canoe was finished and christened the "Bunyip," possibly not the best choice of name if nomen were to be omen, seeing that the bunyip which had recently been sighted in these parts was believed to be a monster dragging its human victims underwater. Was it a crocodile, an ancient creature long believed to be extinct but which had somehow survived, or a giant platypus? No one knew. There had been countless reports—most of them conflicting—since the beginning of the century. He was sure of only one thing: the bunyip hadn't caused his canoe to capsize. That had been his own mistake, just as much as the loss of his shoes.*

*It was late in the afternoon, the sun was still strong, drying him off quickly. From the short stretch of beach, he could see the faint shape of the canoe just underneath the trees that had made him capsize. The river was maybe six feet deep, so it would be possible to haul it to the surface. But how was he going to paddle out of there? Both paddles had drifted downstream, and it would take him forever to carve new ones. Oh well. The frying pan was still there, perhaps he could try to paddle a bit with that.*

*First, however, he would have to retrieve the canoe. He took off all his clothes, spread them over some branches, and walked back into the river. The current wasn't very strong. The fallen trees and their underwater snags formed a sort of weir that slowed it down. He dived under, grabbed hold of the front of his "gum," and started dragging it into shallower water.*

## CHAPTER 2
### SCHNAPPSIDEE

"THANKS FOR THE alarm clock, Dad. A symbolic gift, I take it?"

"Let's call it a wake-up call. Wouldn't you like to join the business? We need someone in the pharmacy."

"Um, yeah, about that, Dad. Sorry, but I have different plans."

His father's eyes were always watery and red.

"What plans?"

"I'm off to Australia."

"That sounds like a *Schnappsidee.*"

Mom and Dad were the product of the war and all the rubble and debris they had grown up in. When he was young, his father had dreamed of becoming an actor. But that was a *Schnappsidee* too, and he soon gave it up to become a pharmacist. He'd wanted Jonathan to study pharmacy, too, so that he could one day take over the family business, but Jonathan had followed his own compass and majored in literature. At university he'd sailed past the great philosophers of the German Enlightenment, almost shipwrecked with the classics, Goethe and Schiller, and finally for the sake of a Master's thesis arrived in a land full of heroic women. Women like Brunhilde in the epic of the Nibelungen, who could throw a rock so heavy that twelve warriors failed to lift it off the ground. Gunther could only win against her and make her his bride with the help of Siegfried, who defeated her while hidden behind the mask of invisibility. He kept reading and rereading such passages. What was the deeper significance of Heinrich Heine's ancient titanic goddess of justice in his *Journey through the Harz Mountains*? Or his

Loreley. He remembered how Frau Grummler had once asked them why the Nazis had forbidden Heine's famous song about the beautiful woman sitting on the rock by the Rhine, combing her golden hair, and singing a powerful melody. The boatmen looking at her would forever be doomed and drown in the river's floods. Of course, the Nazis forbade the song because Heine was Jewish. But was the Loreley some kind of Venus figure? What was it with people disappearing inside mountains, the children of the Pied Piper, or men being lured there by some beautiful goddess? And was this unique to German culture? Didn't Odysseus's resistance to the sirens while tied to the mast of his ship have something to do with this? He'd been discussing questions of myth, landscape, and literature with his father, who had a keen intellectual interest in such things, even if he didn't think there was a future in pursuing them. When he had been Jonathan's age, there had been no time to think about aesthetic questions. He had needed to get a paying job as quickly as possible. In a way, Jonathan understood this, but the times had changed, things were easier now. Some *Auszeit*, time out, as the Germans called it, a gap year away from the pressures of the fatherland, would not hurt him.

"Why Australia? What's there?"

Mom got up and started clearing the table.

"Opportunities, Dad. But, more importantly, I'll be able to grow there."

Dad shook his head.

"Opportunities. You have those right here. There's enough work in the pharmacy to keep it all together."

His eyes had taken on a strange sheen.

"It's a solid business, you know. We have been living off it quite well."

He was right, of course. Owning a pharmacy in a German spa town with its steady stream of ailing patients was like sitting on top of a gold mine. The house in town, a vacation home in the Bavarian Alps: hadn't it all come from Dad's daily drudgery?

The years had clearly left their mark on him. Nearing retirement after decades filled with twelve-hour days, he was severely hunched. He had lost at least five inches over the years.

"Please, Papa. Stop it with the pharmacy. It's not for me. Dealing with people all day long telling you about their health problems. I am sick of all this illness around here. And I just don't see myself behind the counter for the rest of my life."

It wasn't his intention to insult his father, but he clearly had.

Mom grabbed the comb, and started straightening out the fringes of the Persian rug. Maintaining impeccable domestic order was her favorite way of dealing with problems.

"Don't worry," he tried to reassure his father later that night. "I know how to support myself. I've always been able to find work over the years."

His words failed to have their desired effect, for there it was once again, that familiar cynical smile playing around his father's mouth.

"Sure," he hissed. "Factory work. Kitchen jobs. Jobs without a future. You never had to stick with any of them for more than a few weeks. Try and do that for life and you'll see the difference. Look at your Uncle Rudi and the way he ended up."

Uncle Rudi was the *enfant terrible* of the family, maybe because he'd never stopped himself from following his instincts. His relations hadn't forgiven him his pursuit of the pleasure principle, least of all Oma Ilse, his own mother.

Dad, on the other hand, had always subscribed to the reality principle.

"How do you propose to pay the monthly rent with that kind of work? Don't forget that for the last seven years I've been paying for your flat and food, and supported you with a check every month."

He had struck a nerve.

"Money. Is that all you ever think about?"

His father turned pale as a corpse. He was fuming inside, but he never lost his composure. Always exerted perfect self-control. A man has to be like a sword, he used to say. It was one of his favorite lines.

"Let me put it this way," he said under his breath, "you have a choice here: either you're on board with me or you pay your own way in future."

It was a night without sleep. In the early morning hours, Jonathan started sorting through things: the tent, the sleeping bag, swimming trunks, a copy of his new degree in literature, you never know, maybe it would come in handy, sunscreen SPF 50, a moleskin journal, and some of the old friends from the bookshelf: Bruce Chatwin's *Songlines*, Robyn Davidson's *Tracks*, Friedrich Gerstäcker's *Journey round the World.*

Only Ludwig Tieck's tales were missing. Uncle Rudi had them.

His uncle did not look so well. His gray beard was a mess, his left arm in a bandage.

"Have the nurses dropped you again?"

"They drop me all the time."

"Arm's broken?"

"In five places. But hey, it's great you're off to Australia. Go find her, your Alice."

*My Alice*—hearing this joyful imperative gave Jonathan a warm feeling at the bottom of his stomach.

"Once you get a steady job and get married you can forget all about it. You'll never be able to leave again. Do it now, boy! Mark my words!"

A married man himself, Rudi sometimes preferred to move on extramarital trails. His mother, Grandma Ilse, was rock-solidly convinced the strange disease he was suffering from was an inevitable consequence of his loose lifestyle. She even thought it was AIDS after reading an article in the *Bild Zeitung*. The wrath of God, they'd called it, *die Wut Gottes*. The spirit of Wotan could be felt everywhere.

"Who's this Ludwig Tieck guy?" his uncle asked him, turning over the little yellow book of fairy tales.

"He's best known for his folk tale *Puss in Boots*. These are his literary fairy tales. The Phantasus collection."

Uncle Rudi had read the book in one sitting.

"The guy in that one story is amazing," he said, obviously in severe pain. "Just runs away into the wilderness and throws his *Spießer* existence, his petit-bourgeois life, to the wind. He's a bit like you, you know. Maybe you're a modern-day romantic," he said, smiling weakly. "Guard it well, that feeling, don't let it slip away. And make sure you don't slide into that awful middle-class quagmire too soon. It's a life full of lies, believe me, my boy, a life full of lies, the middle-class dream, it's a sham that'll lead to a rude awakening if you've ever dreamed of more."

Then he used his healthy arm to slip a hundred Deutsche Marks into his nephew's jeans pocket.

When Jonathan hugged him good-bye Rudi emitted a small cry of pain.

"Don't let them break all your bones," Jonathan said.

Rudi winked and answered under his breath: "Don't worry. Even if all my bones break in this confounded clinic, one will make a stand to the bitter end." It was his sort of humor. Humor as the last weapon against the playful cruelty of the Gods.

Home again, Rudi's money found a place next to the ticket in the back pages of *The Songlines*, where Chatwin quotes everyone who's ever said anything about nomads. At five a.m. the next day Dad's new alarm clock did a remarkable job, but it wasn't coming along to Australia.

# CHAPTER 3
## SEHNSUCHT

Gender: feminine—literally: the addiction (*Sucht*) to stretch one-self (*sehnen*) toward something or someone; in other, less dramatic words: yearning, longing.

"WHAT'S THE PURPOSE of your visit?"
She was leafing through his passport.
"You realize you're not allowed to work."
"I know. I just—"
She looked up, sternly.
"Just what?"
"I just want to go walkabout."
He had been reading about this quintessential Australian rite of passage on the thirty-hour flight. Going walkabout: it meant following a personal songline.
She looked at him skeptically. "Walkabout? Where? What for?"
"Up the coast and into the outback. For a mystic experience."
"A what?"
"A mystic experience."
"Well, mate, you're certainly an optimist."

After checking into a backpacker's hostel on Victoria Street he strolled down to the Royal Botanic Garden. The cool clear air held a promise of summer. Snow-white cockatoos with yellow hoods were playing in the trees and walking proudly over neatly manicured lawns. Behind the shells of the Opera House, the black silhouette of the bridge spanned the evening sky. He sat down on the steps in front of the opera and drank milk from a two-liter tetra pack. Robyn Davidson had got it right, he thought: there were moments around which your entire life was turning—small flashes of intuition signaling to you that for once you've done the right thing. A moment of pure and uncomplicated trust.

They were seven in the hostel room, and at least one was always snoring. Every night the wee-hour toilet runners would turn on the fluorescent room lights. There were those who partied until three in the morning, not just on weekends, but every single night. They had a habit of breaking into the room as if they owned it, throwing up in the sink and passing out on the floor right next to their bunks.

There were cockroaches, too, he could feel them on his shoulders at night. A medium-sized one sat right next to him, moving its antennae. Were these hostel roaches other travelers who had stayed too long? He was about to kill it when he spotted a tiny exemplar right next to it. Her son maybe. Possibly her only child, he thought, and gave up his murderous instinct.

Peter, one of his roommates, was usually up first and off to the kitchen to brew a cup of tea. On weekdays he put on a suit and a tie, packed his leather briefcase.

"You must be a travelling salesman."

"An accountant," said Peter. "I live here."

"How long have you been here?"

"Over a year."

They called him the Kiwi, but he was also a mole. Far away behind his bottle-bottom glasses Peter's eyes were in a different world. He took his specs off for a moment to scratch the arch of his nose. His bulging eyes sprang forward, large and sore around their lids.

"Why the hostel? With your job, couldn't you afford an apartment instead of roughing it with six backpackers?"

His answer was quick. No doubt people had asked him this before.

"I've no time to travel but being here makes me feel like I'm on the road. It's nice to hear all the travel stories people tell each other. A vicarious kind of life, I know, but I prefer that to being stuck in a lonely apartment all by myself."

The others in the room gossiped about him because his bed was dancing at night, the Kiwi moaning and gasping with the images of untold fantasies. Jonathan talked to him almost every evening in front of the kitchen lockers that contained their supplies, while usurping the entire stove, the beefy Brits were cooking their steak, or some gigantic fish.

Sydney was a money trap. His dollars turning into cents. He stuck stubbornly to his staple diet of two slices of multigrain, spread of Philadelphia cheese and a couple of tomato slices, followed by a few generous swigs from the tetra pack of two-liter milk. Six-hundred dollars was all he had left. The hostel was paid for two more weeks, but without a job his days down under were numbered. What a fool he'd been back home, marveling at George Orwell's descriptions of his days as a beggar in Paris and London.

"What will you do if you run out of money?" Peter looked concerned. "Go home?"

"No way. I'll stay here."

"Are you legal?"

"Not really. I'm on a tourist visa. In six months I have to leave, maybe go to New Zealand, before re-entering for another six months."

But all wasn't lost yet. After dinner, he'd stroll over to the public library, the one next to the hospital with the pig statue outside it: *il Porcellino*, who had cousins in Florence and Munich, all their good luck snouts rubbed golden from too much touch.

With their familiar smell of books, their silence, and the young women engrossed in homework and playing with strands of hair, libraries were a *Heimat*, his natural home. But he didn't go there to read. It was seven p.m. People were leaving, getting their stuff out of the lockers, their metal doors almost all open by now. He looked around a couple of times to check that nobody was watching, then quickly let his fingers wander surreptitiously from one plastic pocket to the next. People leaving the library were distracted, he thought; mentally they were still inside their books, so there was a good chance that they forgot to pick up their deposits. Luck was on his side: once

again he found four golden dollar coins, their kangaroos skipping
happily toward him. It was enough to re-stock on German multigrain, Philadelphia, and tomatoes. At least he didn't need to go out
and shoot a cockatoo the way Gerstäcker sometimes did for want of
better meat.

*The night he lost his shoes, he should have merited more than cockatoo.
It was a massive retrieval action. He had to plunge underwater several
times before he was able to grab hold of the rump in such a way that he
could move it onto the shore. Fortunately the frying pan had got stuck
inside it, and not disappeared in the river. He started ladling the water
out of his vessel. It took him close to an hour, while all that time the
kookaburra never stopped laughing at him. He couldn't see it, it was up
there in the gum tree, well out of sight, and laughing demoniacally at the
stupidity of the German adventurer. He would have loved to stop that
mockery with a good shot from the rifle, but he killed himself a cockatoo
instead, and roasted it over the fire. He detested the meat of cockatoos,
but sometimes he just had to make do. Duck was still his favorite among
the fowls. A black swan here or there had also crossed his path, and he
had made short business of it. Overall, the food wasn't the problem. Of
course, it wasn't as good as back in Arkansas, where he'd lived year after
year killing deer and bear. He quite liked the taste of kangaroo: it wasn't
as dry as venison, more like a mix between beef and buffalo. Plenty of
game around here, he thought, no, that wasn't the problem, but walking
without shoes . . . He wouldn't last more than two miles.*

*Fortunately, the canoe was salvaged. It still seemed river worthy, at
least until he reached the next settlement. There had to be one along the
river; people always settled close to rivers, so it was just a matter of time
before he'd reach one. He'd be all right, he told himself. He'd been in
worse situations. Crossing the Andes in winter had nearly done him in.
Here at least, there was game and water. The situation wasn't hopeless.*

*He woke up in the middle of the night, when a volcano erupted just
beside him. It was a dream, but based on reality. The stump of the tree he
was sleeping next to had caught fire, burning away so brightly it looked
like a volcanic eruption.*

*The next morning greeted him with clear blue skies and screeching
cockatoos all around. He packed up the blankets. Too bad, he thought,*

*that beautiful serape from South America had also been claimed by the
river. Then he pushed the canoe back into the river and continued downstream, using his frying pan as paddle.*

"I found you a job," Peter said one evening. "The Sheldon Hotel's
looking for telemarketers to sell membership cards: ten dollars an
hour plus seven dollars commission for each card sold, cash in hand,
no strings attached. If James asks you whether you're legal just tell
him you're on a working holiday. That's all you need to say. He won't
probe. They're looking for people right now."

At nine o'clock sharp the next morning Jonathan entered suite 207 of
the Sheldon. James was slick and British. He reminded Jonathan of
James Steerforth, David Copperfield's debonair friend.
    "What are you?"
    "Still human, I hope," he said, thinking of roaches and
metamorphoses.
    "Are you legal?"
    "On a working holiday."
    It worked. All travelers from the Commonwealth were entitled
to a working holiday, and Jonathan's strange ability to mimic a range
of UK accents had obviously fooled James Steerforth.
    He sat down at one of the two dozen tables partitioned off from
each other by thin plywood walls, the phone right in front of him
and next to it a writing block, pencils, phone book, and at eye level,
on a piece of cardboard:

Good morning. My name's . . . with the Sheldon Hotel. I'm calling
with an invitation for the director of your company. Would that be
you? Could you put me through to him? Today I would like to invite
you to take out our Sheldon Platinum Privilege Membership. We
invite a limited number of business professionals to enjoy the exclu-
sive advantages of all our Sheldon Hotels in Australia, New Zealand,
and the Fijis. As a member you will receive the Sheldon Platinum
Privilege Card which entitles you to twelve complimentary meals in
all of our thirty-eight excellent restaurants in Australia, New Zealand,
and the Fijis, with no restriction to the price of the meal. We only

expect that you bring one guest. So if two people dine you will pay only half the bill, if three people dine a third of the bill will be subtracted. One person will always dine for free. You can use this card for any meal in any of our thirty-eight excellent restaurants in the South Pacific. The Sheldon Platinum Privilege Card also entitles you to five hotel room coupons. With each of these coupons, the room rate will be reduced by fifty percent in each of our hotels in Australia, New Zealand, and the Fijis. The best thing about this card, however, is that it is fully transferable, so that your friends, family, or business partners can use it as well. The membership fee is $160 and the card expires thirteen months from now. I would also like to mention that the room coupons have no expiry date. Mr. ———, it is our privilege to welcome you as a member to our Sheldon Platinum Privilege Card. Can I confirm your membership?

On his first day, he sold two cards in four hours. The first person he called bought it right away. Midway through the reading, he gave up his credit card number and said, stretching his vowels:

"Yeah, that seems like a useful thing to have."

"Wouldn't you like to know the details?"

"I think I got the message, mate."

The success went to Jonathan's head. He barely took notice of what the next person yelled at him:

"Nah, mate, can't use that sort of thing. I always eat at fish-and-chip shops."

"Good morning. My name's Jonathan Valendas with the Sheldon Hotel. I'm calling with an invitation for the director of your company. Would that be you? Could you put me through to him?"

"You're speaking with *him*," replied a female voice before she hung up.

"I'm calling with an invitation for the director of your company. Would that be you?"

"Unfortunately not."

Click.

"I'm calling with an invitation for the director of your company.

Would that be you?"

"No, it wouldn't."

Bugger off.

"We only expect that you bring one guest. So if two people dine, you'll pay only half the bill, if three people dine a third of the bill will be subtracted. One person will always dine for free."

"Does that mean if I eat lobster and my husband orders a little soup, my lobster is complimentary and he'll have to pay for his soup?"

Her name was Andrea. This was their fifth conversation. She always cut short his sales pitch with "The boss is out, you'll have to call back," before engaging in small talk, obviously bored stiff with her job and happy to pass the time any way she could. He had immediately detected her accent.

"Where are you from," she asked him.

"A small town near Hannover."

"O, ja? Which one?"

"Bad Norndorf."

"Really? I'm from Lauenau."

They had grown up five miles from each other. She seemed very moved and was obviously missing Germany a great deal.

"You should come over and have dinner with us. Meet my husband, Bob. He's a cartoonist, Australia's best. What about tonight even? We're having a barbie."

Their house was on Bourke Street. Andrea was about five years older than Bob, a skinny man in his thirties with graying hair and no shortage of nervous energy.

Bob sized him up through troubled eyes.

"What brings you to Australia," he asked, throwing three steaks on the grill. Deep furrows dropping from his nostrils and bracketing a small mouth that sat like a hyphen on his long face.

"I'm emigrating. Immigrating."

"How does that work?"

"Not easily. I need to find permanent employment with a company that will sponsor me."

"Sounds complicated. You know the best way to become an

Aussie?"

"Surprise me."

"Marry an Aussie girl. Can I pour you some red?"

Bob was a cartoonist. He painted people in the public eye whose physical oddities he was exploiting. His crayons and brushes were like guillotines executing Australia's rich and famous. He turned them into strange hybrids, half human, half animal, hideous creations more satyr than man. If one of his victims had a nose that was slightly too long, Bob would wave his magic brush and lo and behold a platypus appeared. If the teeth of a celebrity approximated the sharpness of those of a predator, Bob would turn her into a Tasmanian devil or a Great White. People struggling with their weight found themselves transformed into wombats. There were kangaroo men, emu women, and echidna men, but Bob also ventured forth beyond the confines of Australian fauna. There were famous giraffes, elephants, and piranhas. The house was spilling over with cartoons and paintings. There must have been hundreds of them.

"Why do you animalize humans?"

His eyes were glistening from the wine.

"Don't you think it's an improvement on humanity?"

They invited him over regularly. Bob was a loner, maybe that's why they hit it off right away. Andrea, on the other hand, sought his company because she was homesick.

"Bob and I got married in Germany five years ago. The civil servant almost ruined our wedding. You know what he said to me?

"'Is he American?' he said.

"'No,' I said.

"'English?' he asked.

"'No.'

"'Well, what is he then?'

"'He's Australian,' I said.

"'You have to be joking,' this guy said, and you know what he said to me then, that dog of a civil servant? He said: 'couldn't you have picked something better? If you got married to a Turk, we'd know what happens when you get divorced; with an Italian too; but with an Australian . . .'"

"He obviously didn't have a sense of humor," Bob said, forking his smoked oysters. "It's one of the most important virtues in Australia. The blacker the better. Gallows humor, you know. It goes back to our past. You can deal with any situation if you have an invincible sense of humor. Those with a sense of humor were the ones who survived."

"Is it true that a foreigner can never mention the convict past to an Australian?"

"Not quite, mate. You're talking about the nineteenth century, when finding out that your family was descended from a convict was what it must be like for a young German to find out that his grandfather was a Nazi. That attitude has changed. Nowadays, Australians are disappointed if they can't boast of at least one convict among their early ancestors. If you want to know more about the history of Australia you should read *The Fatal Shore* by Robert Hughes. That's one of the best accounts of the early years. The Australia he describes was pure hell. And Norfolk Island was the worst. It was a place where all life died and all death lived. Hell on earth, but in a place that looks like paradise. Everyone was scared of Norfolk Island. You know what they did there? They pulled straws. The one who got the shortest was killed first. Of course everyone wanted the shortest. And you know how they got killed there? They had to be clubbed to death by their own mates. If you really want to know about Australia, you should read that book."

"This country has become too small for me. I'm much more than a cartoonist. I'm an artist, but you know how it is for a prophet in his own country. I should probably go to America."

He kept pouring wine.

"Isn't it enough to be one of the best cartoonists in Australia?"

"I'm not sure of it. What do you do when you realize that your art isn't really appreciated? You have to seek new horizons. The other day I stepped in some dog shit on Oxford Street. Later, when I cleaned my shoe, I noticed there was a piece of paper stuck to it with one of my cartoons on it. That's precisely what happens to the work of a cartoonist in Australia. To be stuck to a fridge door means as much to the cartoonist here as being displayed in the Louvre means to a painter in Europe."

He opened another bottle. And he must have read my thoughts, for he said:

"My various attempts at giving up the booze have all failed so far. The other day I went to a doctor because of another little problem. One of those German doctors with the typical you-should-worry-a-little-bit-more-about-your-health attitude. He asks me whether I've been drinking. 'Of course,' I said, 'who hasn't?' 'How much,' he wants to know, and I said to him: 'well, a fair bit.' 'What do you mean by that,' he says, 'what's a fair bit?' 'Well, a fair bit,' I said, 'a fair bit's a fair bit.' 'Do you mean a lot?' he says. 'Yeah, about that much,' I said. He's losing his patience with me and barks: 'Well, please tell me now how much you've been drinking. Is it two schooners a day?' 'Two schooners?' I said. 'You've got to be joking! That's how much I spill every day.'"

"What are your plans?" Bob asked one evening.

"I'm heading for the interior."

He smirked. "Interior of what? Uranus?"

"The outback. Alice Springs and beyond."

"That's quite bold," Bob said. "Are you sure you want to do that? It's a terrible place. How're you going to travel?"

"I'll hitchhike."

His eyes became as wide as a lemur's. For a moment he looked like one of his cartoons.

"That's lunacy. Haven't you heard of the guy who kills hitchhikers? He's already butchered a few of you Germans. They were found disemboweled. You're the only ones stupid enough to go hitchhiking in this country. And if that psycho doesn't kill you, the animals will. This is the most venomous country on the planet, mate. The possibilities of dying are endless: spiders, snakes, dehydration, heat stroke, psychotics, you name it. I wouldn't go, if I were you. If I were you, I'd stay here and start dating Aussie women in Sydney."

He was getting quite worked up about it.

"Let me tell you a story: I once drove from Alice Springs to Townsville. It's a murderous stretch. Nothing to see for thousands of kilometers. Every time a road train was coming my way I put my hand on the windscreen so it wouldn't burst in my face. Finally, the bloody thing broke. My face was badly injured, but there was nothing I could do, I was in the middle of nowhere. Whenever I saw a car in the distance, I'd pull over and park sideways to wait for it to pass. It was bloody hell, mate. When I finally got to the hospital in Mount Isa these two drunks come limping in. One of them is holding a gigantic bag of ice on his face. When he pulled it aside, I almost had to part the tiger. One of his eyes was missing and half his jaw was gone. Of course, he asked to be treated right away. Can't blame him, can you? Wouldn't you want to be treated right away if your eye was hanging from its optical nerve all the way down to your Adam's apple? 'What's happened to you,' the nurse asked him. Of course, he can't talk with the broken jaw and the pain and all that, so his mate answers for him. 'Pub fight,' he says. 'His name, please,' says the nurse, 'address.' The one-eyed fella starts howling and writhing in pain, but she doesn't seem all that impressed. 'Profession,' she goes on asking his mate. 'Has he been here before? If he hasn't been here before, how come he didn't bring his insurance card?' I'm telling you, you'd better avoid the pubs out there. And the hospitals, if you can."

Bob drained his glass.

"What is it that drives you Germans out there? It's almost completely flat, and nothing grows there. People just disappear. Haven't you seen *Picnic at Hanging Rock*? That's not an exaggeration. I'm telling you, we just don't belong there. People die fast in Australia, and you know what: Germans die first."

"What?"

"Germans die first."

"Why's that?"

"You guys overdo it."

He walked over to the bookshelf.

"Here, mate. Let me give you this one for the road. And take this to get yourself a bus ticket."

He handed Jonathan one hundred dollars and a book entitled *A Thousand Ways to Die Down Under: A Natural and Historical Account.*

The next day he was so hung over he slept through most of the bus trip up north. Every now and then he opened his eyes to see quiet lagoons, giant eucalypts, and wild horses galloping alongside the bus north of Byron Bay. The landscape was dappled by myriads of red and purple blossoms, dark pink rhododendrons, banana plants and tall palm trees on fenceless meadows. He never saw the world's longest fence, the famous dingo fence, built entirely for the purpose of pest control.

# Chapter 4
## *GEMÜTLICHKEIT*

. . . defies translation.

Coziness? Not quite. The concept is unique to German culture, its middle-class comforts smacking of beer steins on solid wooden tables, big feather beds, and Christmas mulled wine, *Glühwein*.

HE WAS FAR from all of this. The room at the Hervey Bay Hostel was the very definition of *ungemütlich*. Antiseptic. It was where he met Alan. Although retired, he insisted on wearing a suit and a tie. He even had a small iron that he carried with him wherever he traveled.

"You sound almost American," Alan said without giving him a chance to explain why. "Why are you in Australia?"

"Looking for someone."

"Aren't we all? You really do sound North American. Don't you just love North America? Thirty years ago I met a Canadian, one of those gorgeous blondes, so I emigrated to Toronto. She came from a very wealthy family, so I proposed to her. She said yes, 'but Alan,' she said, 'I'll never go to Australia with you.' 'OK,' I said, 'we'll stay in Canada,' and that's precisely what we did."

Alan was a masterful self-labeler, a Buddhist, a mountain man, a mystic, and a Marxist, all at once.

"I believe that all people are equal." His forehead furrowed into deep lines.

"First of all we're all people before we're anything else. Wouldn't you agree? Take *me*, for example: I'm an academic. I wrote a doctoral thesis in Canada about the inequalities of the Canadian education system. It's a system that favors private schools. The top owners in

Canada all come from six private schools. A system that perpetuates the eternal chasm between the classes, don't you think?"

He put a white shirt on the hostel's ironing board and started working on it.

"I sent all my kids to a private school, but they flunked out of it. Taught me quite a lesson, my kids, taught me quite a lesson."

"Are you here on holiday?"

"Looking for my son."

"Is he missing?"

"He called from Perth. Said he'd never come back to Canada. That was about a year ago. Wanted to stay in Australia for good and marry the pretty blonde he told his mother about. The boy's twenty-one. I said to myself: that can't be it. Get married at twenty-one. You've got to be joking."

"My father would never do this."

"Do what?"

"Search for me."

Alan looked at him intensely, lost in thought.

"He may one day. You never know."

Dad was not the world-travelling kind. From his north German exile, he was forever longing for his Bavarian home. He had never been to Berlin and only once to the North Sea. He travelled in different ways. He would sit at the grand piano playing melancholic melodies. That was how Jonathan remembered him best, moist eyes over his impromptu compositions. And as for travelling, he'd say the wise man sits in his armchair by the window and knows the world.

Alan rolled up his sleeves and kept ironing.

"Been on the road for quite a while now. But I've only been combing the fringes of this vast continent. Well, I suppose he'll come home on his own one day. Maybe sometimes we need to let our children roam. Anyway, it's time to go back to North America soon. I just bought some property, 2.6 acres on the Egg and I Road on the Olympic Peninsula. Beautiful place. You ever been out there? Gotta take care of the property. I don't care what people say about the States. Canada, Australia, they're nothing like the US. I'll spend six months there every year, on my property in the Egg and I Road, the other six months I'll be in Baja. I need solitude. Space."

"And your wife?"

"Oh, she doesn't want to live like that. She'll stay in Toronto where she has her friends, her social life. I've had enough of that. I'm a mystic. I'll found a monastery in Baja. I'll practice yoga. Paint. Write. Mountains. I need mountains. Mountains humble me. People say I need to be humbled. Do you think I need to be humbled? They say I'm too arrogant. Too self-involved." He chuckled. "They may be right."

"So you won't see your wife anymore at all?"

"It doesn't bother me. I've seen enough of her the last twenty-five years."

He told the man about his plan to cross Fraser Island on foot. Alan thought it wasn't reasonable.

"Why would you want to do such a thing?"

"It's training for the outback."

He did not mention that Alice had told him about the island, and how much she loved it there, especially the jewel of a lake at the heart of it. Lake McKenzie: it had been on his mind for years.

"I'd never want my own son to do that. Why don't you rent a nice air-conditioned jeep and drive to Lake McKenzie? Everything you need: water, forest, quiet, and good spirits. But make sure you don't lose sight of the jeep. You could lose it forever. People get disoriented out there. Only takes a minute. They walk in circles and die only a few feet from their cars. And make sure you don't put your foot in the ocean. You can swim in Lake McKenzie, but whatever you do, don't swim in the sea. Go see the shark show here in town, and you'll know what I mean."

He called home the next morning. Maybe Alan made him briefly see himself through his father's eyes. They hadn't talked since he left, but he'd sent a postcard from Sydney. His father made no mention of it. One of his heart valves was almost closed. The doctor suggested surgery. He didn't want the surgery. His voice sounded tired and Jonathan could tell that the question of his return was pressing his father, although it didn't pass his lips.

"You should get a water container," said the kid in the store. "People die from dehydration out there. You can keep filling it up from the lakes. But watch out which lake you take it from. McKenzie is fine."

There were water containers ranging from two to fifty liters. "Why don't you take this one here," the kid suggested. "It's the cheapest." The kid spoke his language. "It's four liters. Just means you have to keep filling it up more frequently."

He also found Australia's cheapest seafood: black and white cans labeled TUNA, the words *and fish byproducts* in small print underneath it, all neatly placed into a pyramid on the bottom shelf.

Fraser Island was only a short ferry ride, and from the pier the trail led straight into the bush.

He was immediately attacked by gigantic horseflies, creatures of astounding beauty but with bites that covered his skin in welts. After twenty minutes of walking in the heavy sand, a car pulled up next to him. It was Rich from Boston, who'd been in the bunk above him at the hostel the night before. The American leaned out of the window: "You look like you could use a break."

The offer was tempting. He hadn't walked more than a mile and the water container was already half empty. He also hadn't expected to find the sand so soft that with each stride he sank knee-deep into the ground. Every single step drove home only one thought: the more you sink into the ground, the more you sweat, the more you drink, the sooner you run out of water, the sooner you die. And Germans die first. Bob's warning fresh on his mind. And Germans did not listen. They had warned Gerstäcker too. He would not listen.

He looked into the back of the Rover. Rich had brought his very own harem.

Almost magnetically, he found himself pulled into their midst, his pack, the plastic bags with the tuna cans, and the water container right between his legs. It was getting tight between Laura, gaunt and English, an Irishwoman called Moira, Susanne and Nicole, two chilly Germans from North Rhine-Westphalia, and a Belgian whose name he forgot instantly. They all smiled a bit except Susanne, who didn't restrain her Teutonic directness. Her knees were almost touching his.

"It's smelly here," she said looking at him. He wasn't aware of it. All he could smell was the soft fragrance of beauty products and sunscreen. Was she referring to his sweat-soaked armpits? He pressed them even harder against his rib cage.

"Couldn't you have thought of this before?"

Thought of what? he thought.

"Thought of what, exactly?" he said.

"That walking on this island is stupid. *Ziemlich blöd*, I must say," she said. "And now you take a spot in our vehicle, for which we had to pay."

Her words swayed the others, who started staring at him with unconcealed hostility. She was right, of course: each of these women had had to pay close to a hundred dollars for a three-day all-inclusive tour, for the car, the camping gear, food, and enough space to breathe inside the vehicle.

"Are you too cheap or can't you afford it?"

He was clearly ruining her vacation.

"Hitchhiking has nothing to do with stinginess. It's a way of life, a culture."

She raised an eyebrow.

"What a strange idea of culture you have!"

When they reached Lake McKenzie, he jumped out of the car and thanked Rich. He couldn't help but notice his T-shirt emblazoned with large red letters:

*Harvard Business School: We Run Things.*

A minute later he was alone again. The bush had swallowed them up, and it felt like he had the island all to himself.

In a place outside human time.

The lake radiates like a sapphire, its snow-white sandy beach forming a half moon round the northern bank. Contrasting with the white sand, McKenzie shimmers in a diversity of hues of blue, from the light shade of the sky reflected in the shallow water close to the beach, through shifting tinges of turquoise, to the dark ultramarine, the color of lapis lazuli, in the middle of the lake.

A yellow-brown dog runs into his field of vision. Its owner can't be far. But the dog has no collar. Stray dogs on Fraser? Better be careful, better watch him. He keeps running up and down along the beach, sniffing in the sand, then looks up holding his muzzle in the air.

Stops and glances around furtively, then steps carefully into the water to drink.

A second collarless dog joins him, then a third.

He sits down in the sand, opens up Bob's book. The ghosts of Fraser Island: In 1836, Captain James Fraser and his wife Eliza were shipwrecked here and captured by Aborigines. One day, while carrying wood, the Captain tripped in the deep sand and was speared down. He died a week later. Eliza spent many more months among her captors until she was rescued and returned to England, where she got rich from telling her tale of captivity in the New World. Initially, English settlers used the island as a sort of natural jail for the indigenous prisoners who were brought here from the mainland. When some of them rebelled against the white settlers, genocide was the answer. The Europeans poisoned their waterholes, mixed strychnine and arsenic into their food, and founded a police force made up of Aborigines who had to go against their own people. Many of them were chased off the land, driven into the sea, where they drowned or were eaten by sharks.

*Little by little he recovered some of the items he had lost to the river: his coat, another blanket, and drifting further downstream he saw another one of his tin boxes, solidly sealed up, so it couldn't fill with water. It got caught by the branches of yet another gum tree that had fallen into the water; otherwise he never would have reached it. It was the one that contained his tobacco, a precious currency in these parts, as he was yet to learn. Despite the loss of his shoes and what little money he had left after Sydney, there was no reason to be downhearted. He hadn't lost his life or been hurt in the accident. His gun was safe, and so was his powder and lead: what more did he want? And yet hunting without shoes had become rather difficult. The ducks he was after heard him from a good distance off, as the old frying pan was making a dreadful noise of splashing; so he needed to go ashore and walk barefoot. His feet weren't used to it. There had been a terrible fire in the Melbourne district that had destroyed all the grass and shrubs as far as the banks of the river, leaving behind nothing but sharp stubble. With every step he took, they went up through his tender skin. He went to bed without any food that night. The next morning, however, after having paddled for a few hours, he saw a fence along the right river bank, and keeping alongside it for another half hour, he spotted in the flickering midday sun the contours of a small settlement. He moored the canoe on a sandbank and headed straight for the buildings. The man who stepped outside and greeted him looked somewhat familiar to him. Had he not seen this man somewhere before? No, it wasn't possible. His accent wasn't Australian either, a recent arrival no doubt from the Old World, so he asked the man where he was from, and was in turn asked the same question. It turned out they had grown up within fifty miles of each other near Hamburg. Their encounter was a very cordial one, as Germans in those days still cherished each other's company when they met fortuitously abroad. But what really added to the great relief and joy of Gerstäcker was that his compatriot happened to be a shoemaker by profession. What greater providence could have been in store for him, he thought, when he heard that this settler in fact had a pair of boots waiting, which somebody had ordered from him but never claimed. Gerstäcker tried them on and, lo and behold—what benevolent angel had ordered these shoes for him—they fit him nicely. But they hadn't been paid for yet, and he had lost all his money to the water. The friendly compatriot insisted on being recompensed, which cost poor Gerstäcker his canoe, the frying pan, and some tobacco. And thus ended his canoe trip and began his long and lonely trek west.*

Now there are four dogs without owners. How can that be? As the cloud lets the sun loose, it dawns on him: these aren't dogs, they're dingoes.

They're all drinking from the lake now, jumping around, playfully biting each other's necks and ears. Suddenly they become aware of him, stare at him in synchrony, and disappear again into the forest.

Around him the microcosm comes to life. Horse flies attack his arms and legs, taking big bites while watching him from myriads of green shimmering facets. Their eyes reflect the colors of the lake. Crawling around his feet are the largest ants he's ever seen, about an inch long, as black as tar, and with massive jaws.

Alone with his life out here. It seems to be worth no more than that of the dingo down there rolling over in the sand. Or the life of one of these flies. All animal eyes are upon him at all times. Is he an intruder to them, or a sensation in a place like this, where very little seems to have changed over centuries? They come from the depths of the bush and look at him with the same kind of terror and awe with which he looks at them and this wonderful place they inhabit. For the first time on this journey, he can feel how vulnerable he is.

A giant bird is flying by singing a somber song.

Soon—all too soon—youth will elude you. After death, this place will be just as it was then and is now. The metal-green flies will still be here: different ones, but identical to the one that has just landed on his arm. Its iridescent colors lose their sheen as a cloud moves before the sun. Clearly, however, he can see it sink its fangs into his skin, in that split second just before the lightning flash and thunderbolt of his flat hand hits home. It falls into the sand, its beauty undestroyed. For a moment, the orchestra of insects grows in a menacing crescendo. A dozen of the giant ants assemble for dinner. Alexander von Humboldt allegedly never killed a mosquito during his travels in the South American jungle. He respected life no matter what its size. To think that a bigger body contains a bigger soul, is it not a fallacy?

The horse fly has been perforated. Huge holes are gaping under its wings.

Something wet suddenly touches his ear. A dingo's nose. He must have been watching him while he was absorbed with the fast motion of physical decay.

Are you to be trusted, old rogue?

They come for him at night as shadows on the canvas of the tent.

Single you are a coward, he thinks, but what tricks will you come up with in a pack? You make me think of European wolves. All the fairy tales Dad used to tell us: Peter and the Wolf, and the one waiting for the girl deep inside the German folktale forest. Is the Australian dingo the equivalent, a mythical archetype, the Jungian trickster and shadow of a subconscious fear? Knowing the wolf is waiting off trail, why does the mother send out her daughter with a basket full of food? Wolves and witches galore. Are they the same in the end? Is the Hansel and Gretel witch the equivalent of the wolf in Little Red Riding Hood? Women consumed by fire, persecuted as werewolves in the early modern age. Burnt on the stake for their deeper knowledge of nature, their powers of healing. Witch, in German *Hexe*, comes from old Gothic *hagazussa*. She is the one who sits on the *hag*, the hedge, the hag on the hag, or on the fence between two worlds, the domestic and the wild. Like the dingo fence keeping the Northerners out and in, the Southerners in and out. All the fences of the world. Between Germany and Germany, the US and Mexico, coyotes crossing at night.

A kookaburra wakes him naturally, watching him intently as he packs up the tent. The dingoes have disappeared. Balancing tuna on a slice of toast, the salty oil giving consistency to it all. Like a bolt of blue lightning, the bird strikes down on the sandwich. For a split second, he can feel his beak touch his palm. The tuna is gone, the kookaburra sitting on a high branch, laughing like a monkey. Laughing at the lonely intruder who is trying to prove what a man he is.

A quick jump into the lake, some deep gulps, fill up the water container, and tighten your shoes. Fifteen kilometers to Lake Wabby, that emerald green lake separated from Fraser's famous seventy-five-mile beach by a sand dune. The sun is only touching the top of the forest, but the heat is already unbearable. By walking in the tire tracks of the four-wheel drive vehicles he is able at least to avoid the deep sand exhaustion, and yet with every step he makes, the many little sips from the water container emerge again with a vengeance as sweat pouring down his face, arms, back, and legs. In droves horse flies assail him, feasting on his blood. A rarely-used smaller path branches off from the four-wheel drive route and is leading deep into the bush. Instinctively, he follows it. It's here that he first notices that he is being followed. He stops and turns around, looks at him looking at him. The yellow ears pricked up, muzzle high, sniffing. The dingo just stands there, waiting, his eyes sharp upon him. He starts walking again, and so does the dingo, about 200 meters behind him. Nature has almost entirely erased this path. There are no tire tracks to flatten and harden the sand. Fallen trees keep blocking his way. Climbing over, ducking under them, he keeps brushing aside webs inhabited by spiders as large as tennis balls with poison-bloated bellies and hairy legs. The trail is like quicksand. With each step it seems as if the earth is trying to swallow him up. Effortlessly the dingo slips through the underbrush, but still in pursuit. He keeps his distance, stops every time Jonathan does to move a branch aside. He feels watched at all times. The branches lying across the path look like snakes. Again and again, he stops to pause and sip from the plastic jug, all the while attempting to keep drying off his glasses with a sweat-soaked T-shirt. How many hours has he been walking? How much longer would it be? When will Mr Dingo give up on him? Is he just waiting for him to give up, so he can pounce on him and strike his fangs into his neck? Divorce yourself from time, mate. And from fear.

It is starting to rain, washing away the sweat, solving the drinking problem. He sits down under a gigantic gum tree, spreads out the tent's rain tarp over him like a roof, and pulls the backpack in between his legs to keep the books dry. An army of black ants has discovered the dry ground around his feet. They quickly conquer his shoes, then their general commands them to start climbing up his naked legs. As the first cohort is reaching the heights just below his knee, they get acquainted with a middle finger flicking them back onto the sandy ground. Hardly have they landed than they start their journey again, just like Sisyphus. The tarp has caught some of the rain, enabling him to fill up the half empty water container again. For the first time that day he finds his center, a sense of calm. Out here the only way to face nature is with a Zen attitude. A small snake escapes into the dry space around him. It shows great interest in the route leading up his legs. It is time to move again. From the corner of his eye he can see the yellow shadow waiting for him to give up, sleep, perish, who knows what his intentions are, is it a predatory instinct that makes him follow or just curiosity? In any case, he won't give up, the dingo teaches him that lesson, propelling him to a higher level of consciousness.

Not seen a single human soul all day. Like an emerald jewel shining in the evening hours Lake Wabby suddenly appears ahead of him, the sky opens up allowing golden rays to pour over its silent water. But the lake is doomed. With each passing day that sand dune separating it from the sea invades it a bit more. One day Wabby will be gone.

So is the dingo, as he steps out of the bush.

He smells them long before he can see them.
Rich and his nymphs are sunbathing lazily on the dune. They stare at him as if they have just seen a spirit emerging from the woods. Susanne, the feisty Westphalian, comes right over. How pretty she is, the golden light playing with her blonde curls, her eyes the same color as the turquoise shades of Lake McKenzie. She looks at him in a strange way:
"Why are you doing this?" Her voice a blend of miscomprehension and admiration.
"Doing what?"
"Why are you running through the bush in this heat instead of enjoying yourself?"
In German she says "instead of making it *gemütlich* for yourself."
"But I *am* enjoying myself."
Fuck *Gemütlichkeit*. Gerstäcker didn't like it either.

He tosses down the pack and plastic bags, slips the sweat-soaked T-shirt off his chest. Tearing himself from her gaze he sprints down the dune and throws himself into the cool, opaque water.

# CHAPTER 5
## *AUFBRUCH*

... has the double meaning of *setting out* and *breaking open*

HE SHOULDERED HIS pack and started walking out of Townsville on the left side of the road. Every time he heard a car approach he turned around, stuck out his arm, and tried to look at the driver. It was the polite way of hitchhiking, supposed to inspire trust. He had seen others just keep on walking, who would never face the driver, thumb casually stuck into the road.

A few cars passed, but then a pickup rolled to a stop right next to him. A middle-aged man under a huge hat, a young man in the passenger seat.

"How far you going, mate?"

"Alice Springs."

"I go as far as Charters Towers. You should take a look at it. It's a very old town."

They drove in silence.

"Only few people go past Charters Towers. You may have a hard time getting a ride."

"I'll try."

"Why Alice Springs?"

"Looking for someone."

The man nodded quietly. He waved a mighty finger at the landscape.

"See those trees, mate? Those are date palms. They're not indigenous. From Egypt. They pull all the water from the ground. Now the government's trying to get rid of them. If you ask me, it's too late."

They cruised through the ancient town of Charters Towers. He dropped him off at the most western habitation, a gas station, then turned back.

"Next town is Hughenden. Quite a ways out there. Be careful. Land's possessed by the devil. Those who tried to lick it have failed. Let me give you two pieces of advice. Make sure you always wear your hat and carry enough water."

He downed a few cans of coke and walked over to the men's room to fill up his water container. FLIP DRY or DRIP DRY: the choices on the toilet doors. In the shade three men keep pummeling a shaky aluminum table with their playing cards. They drain one can of XXXX after another, then squeeze the life out of them, and throw them carelessly into the sand. Deeply tanned, they scan him suspiciously. He pulls down the akubra, grabs the plastic bags with the tuna cans, the water container, and starts walking west along Flinders Highway, eyes glued to the boiling bitumen.

Road of dead rabbits.

Song of their sweet sickly smell.

Horizons flickering in the corner of his eye, fat clouds traveling east. Being footloose has always exhilarated us. It is associated in our minds with escape, from history, oppression, law, and irksome obligation. In absolute freedom the road has always led west.

After three kilometers he reached the big green sign spelling out the deadly distances.

Hughenden 250 KM
Mount Isa 760 KM
Tennant Creek 1440 KM
Darwin 2370KM
Alice Spings 1950 KM

Nothing else in between?

Place bags and water container in the sand.

Throw off the pack.

Stretch.

A mild breeze visits his soaked back.

This had to be the best spot for hitchhiking. Whoever came by here would have to stop from sheer compassion. He sat down on his backpack.

An hour passed and with it three cars.

*As Byron once said, there is pleasure in the pathless woods. Following the course of the Murray, however, he noticed how dry the land was all around him. As hard as horn it was, cracked everywhere by heat and drought. Walking mile after mile he did not see a single blade of grass. Getting good water was a problem. The small lagoons and billabongs lining the river contained only foul smelling water, from which hundreds of cattle had died and now lay scattered around the landscape. Even the dingoes shied away from eating the decomposing cows and sheep, although now and again they would steal up to the dying animals and tear a chunk of flush from them, leaving them in agony, their painful mooing and bleating to be heard for many miles.*

*The water situation had been dismal, forcing him periodically to make his way to areas where the river was flowing rapidly, ladle water from it with the small cooking pot he had been able to salvage after the boat had sunk, then build a fire and boil the water. On his belt, still from the days in Arkansas, he carried a pouch made of deer hide that he could fill with water. He'd boil the water and fill up that pouch. When he got to where the Edward River flows into the Murray he found land that he thought the best for sheep farming in all of Australia. The reason for this was a small plant that grew everywhere, it was called salt bush, and the taste of its saline leaves was pleasant not only to the sheep but also to Gerstäcker, replenishing the loss of salt from his constantly sweating body. The other plant in abundance here was pig's face, a rhizomatic plant that grew along the ground like a vine, some of its leaves salty, some bitter, some sweet. It became his staple for many days, an ideal condiment to his habitual diet of meat. For years, in Arkansas, he had lived almost exclusively on venison.*

*Whenever he reached a sheep station he was surprised how hospitably he was received by the settlers. He became convinced there was no country in the world where hospitality was carried to a greater extent than in Australia. The shepherds would never turn anyone from their doors, nor would they accept any sort of remuneration for their generosity, in fact they seemed insulted whenever he suggested paying them for the shelter and food they provided.*

*It was the end of May, and he had been following the Edward River for a few days now. It seemed that the hospitality he had experienced everywhere was the product of a wide-spread knowledge of the uncertainty travelers faced wherever they went. The shepherds he stayed with warned him about the dangers lying ahead, about hostile tribes, warring among each other, and having frequently attacked white travelers. Recently several travelers had been killed, one of them had even been found staked to the bottom of the river. He was cautious therefore, as he kept walking west, back along the Murray, in country where the mallee tree grew, a kind of eucalypt that had water in its roots, thus offering prime territory for human habitation.*

*One day he encountered a group of about twenty. They were obviously on the war path, painted in white and red clay and armed to their teeth. Each of the men carried at least one spear in addition to two types of boomerang, the kind that was curved in such a way that it would return, and those that did not. On the wrist of the right hand hung the little war club and slung over their shoulders they had long shields. Upon seeing him, two of the younger men split from the group and disappeared into the bush. As he approached the larger group, he cocked his gun twice to let the noise of the springs be heard and kept walking on. The case grew rather too exciting to be pleasant. They were obviously debating his presence, most likely trying to decide what to do with him. He wasn't sure if, in the case of an attack, they were after his gun or his kidney fat, his "butter" as they would call it. In any case, he was determined to give them neither.*

The station wagon was stuttering to a slow halt as one of the wheel caps detached itself and, ignoring the silence, set off on its own, trying to roll back to civilization. Without success, since after a few meters it started dancing wildly round its own center until it came to lie flat on the road.

"Where you goin' mate?"

"How far you going?"

"Mount Isa."

They were studying each other's faces. His station wagon did not inspire trust.

"Get on in, mate! Name's Adam. What's yours?"

There was no space in the car, the view from the rear mirror completely blocked by suitcase, boxes, a complete household it seemed, and the front seat full of cookie crumbs immediately attacking his thighs. Between his feet on the passenger side stood Adam's esky. It looked as if it had been chewed on by rats and contained nothing but ice cubes, no food, no drink. McVitie's were all Adam seemed to crave: they were spread throughout the vehicle, some of them in good condition, others half-nibbled on, most of them ground into crumbs. But what were the ice cubes for, he wondered, considering Adam had nothing to drink?

Adam was a rigger from Cronulla.

"What do you rig?" he asked him.

"Right now I'm rigging a new life, mate."

"Moving into the interior?"

"Yeah, mate. I thought it was a good idea to be away from Sydney.

He grabbed some of the ice cubes from the esky and tossed them clink clonk into the dirty glass on the dashboard. Within minutes they were dissolved. Adam grabbed the glass, greedily downed the ice-cold water and refilled it.

After six hours, four hastily injected McVitie-induced digestive breaks, and hundreds of kilometers of space, they reached a small town. The sun was already low as they filled up the tank. Adam asked the Texaco man to check the engine. While he and the mechanic were engrossed in skeptic inspection, Jonathan was making sandwiches on the car roof. It was so hot the limp slices of wonder bread were getting nicely grilled. Time to use up the Philadelphia cheese and the tomatoes, both had relinquished their freshness some time ago. Adam renewed his supply of ice cubes and McVities. He did seem to relish the sandwiches, stuffing them into his face without chewing.

"You wanna make sure those flies don't land on your sandwich because once they start shitting out larvae and maggots it's too late. Let's go have a pint, mate."

Walking through the beer golden haze of the evening they entered the local pub, which at this time of day was full of people.

Those sitting at the bar were half naked, their watery eyes glued to the beer taps right in front of them. An orchestra of drinkers directed by a red-cheeked woman sailing from tap to tap, pouring pint after pint. Their bodies moving in slow motion, their shoulders drooping forward. In rapid succession, Adam drained a few schooners, then ordered pints for both of them.

"So there's no work for you in Sydney?"

"There is, but I wanted to get out. Just got divorced. My wife, ex-wife, I should say, is getting married to a banker. Makes more money, that bloke. She was tired o' me not making enough."

He looked around nervously.

The guy next to Adam turned around and asked him where he was from, his voice like song reaching higher levels toward the end of the question.

Adam said: "Redfern, mate."

"You two a couple?"

Adam stared straight ahead, taking a large swig from his glass.

"Did yous not hear me?"

"We're just mates."

"Why don't you go back to where you come from? People like you aren't welcome here."

The conversation around them had ceased. They drank up, paid, and left.

"Why did you tell them you're from Redfern? Aren't you from Cronulla?"

"That was on purpose. You never tell anyone out here you're from Sydney."

"But isn't Redfern a part of Sydney?"

"Sure, mate, but it's not upper-class Sydney, like Cronulla. They know that out here, so if I say I'm from Redfern I sort of express my solidarity with them."

As they were cruising out of town a woman staggered into the road. She waved at them. Apparently the only friendly soul in town, so he waved back. As they got level with her she screamed through the open window:

"You woofter bastards, you bloody woofter bastards!"

At least the night bid them a warm welcome.

"Here, hold on to the steering wheel for a moment."

Adam plunged into the wires of his radio just above the gas pedal.

"To make it work you need these two cables here, the blue one and the red one. Then you peel back some of this plastic coating here and tie the copper wires around each other. Just like this. See?"

INXS blasted into the night: *Holden wrecks and boiling diesels steam in forty-five degrees.*

The windows were all down so the wind could chase away the various smells trying to settle inside the car.

"Dead animal," said Adam. How did he know? Was the smell of a dead animal different from a dead person? The longer the cheesy odor lingered the bigger the corpse. But the dead-animal guessing game helped pass the time: one minute for a bunny, three for a roo, passing a dead cow the smell lasted for five minutes. Did a roo smell different from a cow or did all animals smell alike once they decomposed? Adam thought there were differences, after all the critters had different diets.

"Smell that?" he said. "Carnivore. Probably a dingo. Definitely not cattle."

"Do the cows find enough to eat out here?"

"I would think that each cow has several acres to graze from. They'll find enough, mate."

"So the farmers share the land?"

"They sure don't. These aren't farms here. They call 'em cattle stations. Some of them are as big as Germany."

"As big as all of it, East and West combined?"

"As big as that. Possibly bigger."

It was around midnight, and they were about 100 kilometers west of Julia Creek. The fuel tank was almost empty. Suddenly, the tire that had initially lost its wheel cap popped, sending them skidding off the bitumen.

"Let's spend the night here, mate."

"Don't you have a spare?"

"Nah, no worries, we'll hitch a ride back to Julia Creek tomorrow, they got fuel and tires."

There had been nobody for many hours. Adam turned off the engine.

The silence was perfect.

Even the high wind that had traveled a long way became a part of it. Making his bed in the back of the station wagon Adam said: "Why don't you sleep on the roof? You're safe up there from anything that might crawl past here tonight."

He took off all his clothes except for the boxer shorts and climbed onto the roof, stretched out and tucked himself in with the breeze as his bed cover. Around him lay the flat black plain and above it a huge starlit sky.

"Better than Germany, isn't it?" came from below. "We have a lot more stars here than you, don't we?"

"Sure." He didn't want to argue with him. But Adam was right. Nine-tenths of the visual field was filled with stars. There were no artificial sources of light anywhere. It seemed as if he was floating through the universe. A complete loss of gravity.

"You must be very happy with your country these days."

"Why's that?"

"Well, with the wall being gone now."

"What do you mean, gone?"

"Didn't you see the images on the news just the other day?"

"What images?"

"Where've you been, mate? The party they had on the wall. The East Germans broke through it. Just a few days ago."

What on earth was he talking about? Suddenly, gravity had him back.

"It was all over the news. Germany reunited. The wall's come down."

"Are you out of your mind, Adam?"

"I think *you* are, mate. You've obviously been on walkabout too long. I reckon we need to celebrate tomorrow."

It must have happened when he was on Fraser Island, swimming in Lake McKenzie, hiking the bush trails to Lake Wabby. For a few days he had been in the dusklands well outside of history. Sure, it had been in the offing when he was still back home. Down there in the South of Bavaria, with all the cars arriving from Hungary, streaming across the Austro-German border near Salzburg. Long strings of Trabis and Wartburgs on the autobahn heading west, then north, to Munich and beyond. Like an ant trail, dreaming of the land of oranges and bananas now wide open. He remembered the young East German who walked into the restaurant where he was having his Schnitzel, sitting down right next to him and staring at him taking bite after bite. Could he buy him a Schnitzel he asked the East German who said yes but no pommes frites, no fries, just a Schnitzel and a slice of bread. He ordered it for him, and that guy wolfed it down in no time, then got up and walked back to his little paper car. He drove off without a word of thanks. But that was all right, they, the West Germans, had owed it to them for all those years of being trapped behind the Iron Curtain.

But the wall gone now? He couldn't envision it. Tears shot to his eyes as he was thinking of his battered home country so very far away. From his bed on the warm tin roof of Adam's station wagon he stretched out his arms toward the stars, nearly touching the Southern Cross.

"You know what a stockman's breakfast is?" Adam asked the next morning. "A piss and a good look around." The tire may have been deflated but not Adam's mood. The McVitie's were all gone and so were the ice cubes, so they had to make do with a stockman's breakfast. The ground which hadn't seen a drop of rain for months thanked them for it. There were no trees, no shrubs, a few termite hills at best.

The first one to pass was a road train, one of those monstrous trucks with three units. It must have taken half a mile to stop.

Back in Julia Creek they got a new tire, some fuel, and invested in the greatest luxury of the outback: five minutes under the shower. He even threw in a couple of Mars bars. This was how they celebrated the fall of the wall.

They got to Mount Isa late that night. A rough town with lots of chimneys and unhappy people trying to drown their grief in cheap alcohol. Sitting under sick-looking gums in whose shade empty beer bottles were piling up.

How was Adam going to rig a new life here?

The next morning, he was ready for his job. They shook hands for a long time.

"Take good care of yourself, mate."

His voice was soft, with a touch of sadness in it. For two full days they had been traveling together, sharing digestive biscuits, embracing the stars, even surviving a punctured tire. He felt a strong bond between them and it must have been the same for Adam. Good luck with your new life here, was all he could think to say.

## CHAPTER 6
### *LEBENSLAUF*

Gender: masculine; course of life, curriculum vitae

Camooweal 188
Darwin 1600
Alice Springs 1180

It took two hours to get a hitch out of town. It was a young guy who didn't talk much except for "I'm droppin you off here" after about an hour of driving. No sooner said than done. A cloud of dust followed him as he was tearing down a dirt track leading to the Gun Barrel Hotel.

Earlier there had been some rain but the ground had soaked it all up. Now the clouds were breaking, and the polished blue showed between white cotton balls. The land was brightly lit. Beautiful but deadly, this Australian landscape was practicing its economy: some low trees on red soil and dead fallen branches like the arms of skeletons, bony hands clutching on to meagre pickings. Shreds of rubber everywhere, instilling a sense of hope in him. Some people seemed to be traveling along this lonely highway.

A hugely bloated cow soon found him. Now and then, the wind changed direction, sometimes shielding him from the stench, but then it came back with a vengeance. He pulled the akubra low onto his face.

Small sips from the plastic jug. The water seemed to go straight to his head and reappeared in small beads soon discovered by flies tiny and swift. When he took off his hat they exploded from him, buzzing around the carcass, before returning for more forehead sips: eat, drink, eat, drink. He had become part of the fly buffet.

Four hours went by. His water supply was nearly gone. Should he walk back to Mount Isa? Seventy pounds in the pack and no water. The thought made him panic for a moment. So he chased it away. There was still the oil from the tuna cans to rely on.

Suddenly, a small dot appeared on the horizon. It got bigger and bigger, slowly, ever so slowly, until it turned into a bright red car. Wildly gesticulating, he saw himself jump into the road. But the car didn't slow down.

Instead it changed lanes.

Passed him.

And was gone again.

*The case grew rather too exciting to be pleasant. It looked as if he had to fight his way through them somehow or find himself staked to the bottom of the river. He hadn't made more than about two hundred meters when he saw the two young fellows who had left their mob make a beeline straight ahead, so that they were bound to meet up with him. Stopping, they seemed to wait for him. Looking back over his shoulder, he saw the rest of the group assemble up on a rock to watch the spectacle unfold below. He did not like the idea of it, but had lived among Native Americans long enough to know that it would be the end of him if he showed any fear. Cocking his gun again and letting it rest in the bend of his arm, he walked leisurely up to the two young men. "You smoke?" said one of them. He said no and kept walking without looking back. He heard them exchange a few quick words and then accelerate their steps to catch up with him again. "You smoke," the young fellow asked again, forcing him now to confront them. No, he said again, whereupon the lad became very impatient, yelling at him that he was telling them lies, so he said very calmly that he did indeed have some tobacco on him, but would only be willing to part with a portion of it in exchange for one their boomerangs. The effect of this proposition was rather strange. They looked at each other, then burst out laughing, whereupon the one he had spoken to exclaimed "Well, well. I give you boomerang!" He started running away from him, then turned around*

*and was brandishing his large curved boomerang over his head. It looked*
*as if he wanted to throw it at Friedrich, who clutched his gun and made*
*the spring of the lock sound.*

Another vehicle was approaching. It did not seem to slow down
either, two people inside, an empty back seat. They started making
a wide berth around him. Imploringly, he threw up his arms, flung
off the akubra, picked it up again, and stroked his beard. Was that
beard the cause of all the distrust? He waved desperately to them as
they were passing him. Sure enough, there was a reaction, or was it
his mind playing tricks on him, they were slowing down now, weren't
they, the metallic blue car moved to the side of the road. Then they
stopped. This was his ride, there was no choice. All caution thrown
to the wind. The serial killer could have been in there for all he cared,
he had to get out of here.

It was a young guy, maybe nineteen, fear written all over his face, a
young woman in the passenger seat. They seemed strangely familiar.
Where had he met these people before? No, it was impossible, but
then again, their clothes, the posture, their faces. He knew their type,
all over the world he could spot a German a mile off. So he immediately addressed them in German:

"*Fahrt ihr nach* Camooweal?"

It was a silly question. Where else could they have gone?

The young man was surprised but obviously relieved at the sound
of his language. His face was starting to relax, and the girl even broke
into a faint smile.

His reply was definitely that of a German:

"You'd have to pay for part of the fuel."

Maybe Germans died first out here, but they were also the first
ones to save you.

"We're from Ingolstadt."

"Ah, Frankenstein."

"Frankenstein?"

"Ja. Frankenstein. Ingolstadt. His lab."

He looked puzzled. "I'm Thomas," he said. "And this is Birgit."

"I've been waiting for five hours, you know. You're only the second car to come by here today. Half an hour ago, this guy in a red

BMW passed me. Accelerated when he saw me."

"Red BMW? Bearded type? He's Swiss. He's been traveling ahead of us for days. Always stops at the same gas stations where we catch up with him. I have no idea what he's doing there for so long, but I think he spends a couple hours under the shower. Beats me how he can get dirty in his air-conditioned BMW."

Thomas and Birgit from Ingolstadt seemed quite happy to have found someone to talk to.

"How long are you here for?"

"I don't know. Maybe a year."

"Just travelling?"

"Looking for someone."

Thomas was a student of computer sciences.

"What do you do for a living?"

The question had to come sooner or later.

"I was a student until recently."

"Of what?"

"Literature."

"Is that why you have so much time now?" They grinned at each other. "What will you do one day, with literature?"

He had ready answers:

"Garner a deeper sense of life."

Thomas's subsequent monologue about the opportunities for students of computer science both in Germany and elsewhere slid by him like a bearded Swiss in a BMW. Sure, some bits here and there may have reached one ear, something about him being nearly finished at university and already getting offers from illustrious companies in Munich and Stuttgart. Thomas noticed Jonathan's inattentiveness and proceeded to make him the target of his predictions, forecasting that studying literature would most certainly lead to lifelong unemployment, that bumming around Australia, even for just one year, would be two nails in anyone's career coffin. Any employer would immediately spot the gap in the *Lebenslauf. Die Lücke im Lebenslauf.* The gaping hole in the CV. Nobody would object to a three-week vacation. But a year? It was professional suicide.

The sunlit landscape was silently gliding past them. For a moment he was yearning to be back out there.

"Who are you looking for?" Birgit asked.

"The love of my life."

It was his second blowout in as many days. He helped Thomas dig the spare from the trunk before distancing himself a little from the car. After all, Thomas was the techie, not him.

There it was again, the sublime silence of the outback.

Surreptitiously, he took a photo of the blue Holden on the red sand under a blue sky and the cumulus clouds. The two Ingolstädters were kneeling in front of their vehicle as if lost in prayer.

In the afternoon they reached Queensland's last settlement: a dozen houses, a caravan in front of each. The gas station was the last building. The sign next to it made you seek instant shelter:

LAST FUEL FOOD AND WATER FOR 300KM

Inside the gas station, which contained a restaurant and a grocery store, a few serious truckers were silently digging into their burgers.

"Anyone going to Three Ways?"

They shook their heads.

The owner of this oasis, a huge man, told him to leave his pack outside.

"Nobody's goin' to Three Ways," he said gruffly. "If you want to buy something let me know, otherwise be on your way."

There it was again, the eternal mistrust with which the sedentary world treats the wanderer.

"Can I fill up my water container?"

"We sell water. Five dollars a bottle." With his massive finger the man pointed at the small Evian bottles next to the door.

"Don't you have tap water in that restroom over there?"

The giant walked over to him, his eyes narrowing:

"Where do you think you are? Do you think we can waste water around here?"

He bought a can of coke and a Mars bar for six dollars and sat down by the truckers. Thomas and Birgit were bent over their Holden, checking its oil level. Gray clouds had moved in again. A few precious drops were falling on this part of Queensland, but hardly more than five dollars' worth.

There was no point in going further that day. The two Ingolstädters also decide to spend the night. Behind the gas station there is a small piece of lawn with a few tents on it. Next to it Queensland's last swimming pool, a sign on its fence:

KEEP OUT. PRIVATE POOL.

Not far from there, another sign:

NO LOITERING.

*Gerstäcker hadn't flinched but stood his ground, which made the young man falter. Lowering his boomerang, he walked back to his friend and put it into the German's hands. They both looked very happy at the receipt of some of his tobacco. Suddenly, a loud cry broke out from the hill. He was convinced that it was the signal for an immediate attack against him, but here he was wrong again. The two young fellows picked up their spears, swiveled around, and ran up toward the others. They were at war with another tribe, and there was obviously something going on over on the other side of the rock that was of more interest to them than a solitary German traveler trespassing on their territory. His breathing became more regular again, and he decided not to hang around but move on out of this area as fast possible.*

Suddenly, he stood right next to him. That barrel of a man. The NO LOITERING sign must have had his name on it. With suppressed aggressiveness, almost whispering, the colossus snarled: "I'd appreciate it if you didn't ask any more people for a hitch around here. The customers don't like it and neither do I." Did this man think that he was going to rob him? But of what? The water from the pool? Under the wafer-thin surface of his politeness his heightened irritability lay barely concealed.

"No worries," he reassured him, "Mind if I pitch my tent?"

His words calmed the man slightly and for a moment he reminded him of Uncle Scrooge, the dollar signs in his eyes.

"Five dollars per tent and one dollar extra for the shower. It runs for precisely six minutes."

Pressing the water container to the shower head it only took a minute to fill up. Maybe it was the five-minute shower that made the difference, but it was probably paying for pitching his tent on the lawn that he was no longer a vagrant but a customer in the eyes of the King of Camooweal. When he walked back into the store, a hint of a smile stole across the man's face. Jonathan politely returned his kindness before directing his attention to the postcards by the door. The best way to get to know a place one has no desire to really get to know is by studying its postcards. Camooweal, Queensland, and its immediate surroundings had three motifs that had attained the status of tourist attractions: a group of horses gathered around a billabong, the ornate verandah of the local pub, and an inconspicuous tree on a flat piece of arid land. The back of the card revealed the tree's location. It stood two hundred miles to the north in a National Park named after it:

Lone Gum National Park.


It was a stormy night. The tent got blown this way and that but did its job. The next morning came brightly and hot. Thomas was up first. He heard him rummage around for a long time before he got up. When he stepped outside, he asked him if he could join them as far as Alice Springs.

"For a third of the gas." It was a predictable reply.

The two Ingolstädters needed an hour to pack up. They were amazingly well prepared. According to patriarchal law, Thomas was in charge of the tent and the sleeping bags, while Birgit looked after the kitchen utensils. He kept unrolling the sleeping bags to re-roll them over and over until they had reached their desired minimal size.

"So they don't take up much space in the *Kofferraum*," Thomas said. "Learned this in the army."

He was glad Thomas didn't ask him about his time in the German military.

The Holden's trunk contained several jerry cans labeled *Wasser* (water) and one labeled *Benzin* (gasoline). Each day, Thomas explained, they prepared three meals on the little gas stove. They had brought almost all their food from the Aldi store back home and had even thought of their vitamins. While Thomas was counting the stakes of the tent, Birgit was peeling two apples. Followed by two oranges. Finally, she filled a pair of plastic cups with water and dropped a fizzy vitamin tablet into each.

Jonathan opened his last can of tuna. The wonder bread looked a bit stale. It was time to use it up. The two Ingolstädters made him think of the words of François, who lived in Helsinki. "There are just too many darn Germans in Finland's forests," François once told him, turning his eyes to heaven the way French people do. "They come up here in the summer, live in their tents for weeks, and hunt down our reindeer." He really did say our reindeer, although he was French. "And you know what's the worst," François said leaning over to him and letting his voice spiral to a level that qualified as shrill: "*Le pire, c'est qu'ils avaient déjà préparé leur sauce.*" The worst was that they had already prepared their sauce back in Germany.

After a few minutes they reached the Northern Territory. The road was flat and completely straight as it had been for days, but the land west of Camooweal filled with even more emptiness. There were no more trees out here, nothing but hard, torn earth over hundreds of miles. Only now and then the straight line of the horizon was ruptured by the cathedrals of the outback: termite hills.

The Ingolstädters loved their little rituals. Precisely every hundred kilometers Thomas stopped the car. He got out, walked off the road a bit, and took a picture of the empty land. If there was a point of interest, say a termite hill or a shrub at KM 192, he kept going for another eight kilometers to stop and once again make a photo of nothing.

"Wouldn't you prefer to bring home a variety of impressions?"

The question irritated Thomas.

"I want to document the subtle changes of the Australian landscape."

"But it's not changing. You have taken the same picture three times now."

"That's precisely what I want to show my people back home: that this landscape is so huge you cannot record any real change over hundreds of kilometers."

"But why don't you just take three pictures in one spot instead of having to stop every hundred K? Or even better: why don't you just take one picture and make three copies?"

They were equally religious about their curve log book. How many curves did the road make from Sydney to Townsville, from there to Alice Springs, then on to Adelaide, on to Melbourne and back to Sydney? Every curve was registered in the curve log book as well as the date, the time of day, and the mileage at which the curve was experienced. Every time they encountered what promised to be the intimation of a curve, they started fighting over the question whether it was or was not a curve. Could the slightest bend in the road be defined as a curve? Or in other words: when precisely did a straight road become a curve? Was Thomas trying to resist all curves?

Passing three suicidal bicyclists: Japanese. "Take a photo!" Jonathan yelled, but Thomas didn't.

Looking at the landscape, it was difficult to see how such empty and flat country could contain beauty. But then again, was anything ever really empty? Was emptiness not just an empty word for something whose fullness wasn't immediately visible, audible, smellable, tangible, and then some? To be thought, felt, or associated? Crossing Australia by plane coming from Germany, he had thought of a painter's palette: from the ultramarine of the ocean over the thin emerald corridor along the coast and the various shades of brown and ochre to the vermilion-red center, an ensanguined ocean with its small black waves. When the sun comes out, the ground traveler's visual field is divided by one straight line, blue above, red below. When clouds move in, the colors multiply: white, gray, blue, bright red, soft brown. Beauty out here evokes itself from the sensation of flatness, distance, from a landscape that calms the senses, softens the emotions. Adalbert Stifter, an Austrian writer and landscape painter of the nineteenth century, thought that the quiet Hungarian *puszta* was preferable to a jagged Alpine mountain panorama. He called it the *sanfte Gesetz*, the gentle law. Stifter would have loved this monotony of lines. And all these wanderers out here follow their own lines through it: Adam, rigging a new life for himself, the King of Camooweal, in pursuit of the vertical line of sedentariness and ownership, and Thomas and Birgit on a straight career path interrupted by a few weeks' vacation on the uncurving roads of Australia. The wind carrying its lonely voice. No kookaburra laughs, no insect hums out here.

At "Three Ways," where Barkly Highway meets Stuart Highway, where the rib joins the spine, there was little to welcome the weary traveler: a few solitary car wrecks that had managed over the years to adapt to the land around them both in form and color, a gas station, the usual KM sign discouraging people to go on, and a stone in memory of John Flynn, the Flying Doctor. With some sadness in his heart, he was thinking of Adam. He had tried several times to demonstrate his knowledge of the dead fauna to the two Ingolstädters by calling out dead cow, dead roo, or dead dingo whenever the wind would waft through the open windows, although they had never spotted a carcass on the flat ground.

Getting out of the Holden, he realized that his tennis shoes successfully united those three smells in them. They had cost twelve dollars, and he had worn them faithfully for two months. Surreptitiously, tying them by their strings, he found a burial ground for them in one of Three Ways's many dumpsters. From the deepest recesses of his pack came a brand-new and completely identical pair. If Gerstäcker had taught him anything, it was never to be without a second pair of shoes.

Tennant Creek.

Gold was found here in 1930. Since then, mining had been the biggest business. Nobles Nob, the richest gold mine of the Northern Territory, was discovered by two men who shared one eye between them. According to legend the town was founded when a beer truck collapsed seven miles to the south and people decided to settle around the stranded amber fluid. The tourist brochure was fifty pages long and full of attractions.

The sky was beginning to brood and music came riding with the wind, galloping toward him, disappearing, then again full-blown.

From the darkness ahead suddenly emerged a brightly lit funfair, its main attraction being a garish auto-scooter rink. The kids of Tennant Creek had gathered here to whirl around in a storm of pop songs competing with the weather. As their scooters collided so did electric vibes, those of the air with those of youth. A tall young girl drew his attention, she reminded him of Alice when he first met her, so young and yet so much taller than everyone else. She had extremely long legs and like the other Aboriginal teens was barefoot and dressed in ill-fitting clothes. After each round she jumped out, ran over to the ticket office, bought plastic chip after plastic chip. Her favorite game seemed to be driving her scooter into that of a whimpering white boy roughly her age. Every time she crashed into him, he lost control of his neck muscles, his head thrown into whichever direction the collision dictated. Screaming in pain, he raises his fist at the girl, and yet just like her he keeps buying token after token to do round after round with the scooter, exposing himself to her attacks.

The next morning they made a stop at Devils Marbles. There it was, the split onion, its halves in the shape of a V. The eggs of the rainbow serpent or the result of lava pressed to the surface where erosion had stripped them of its layers like onion skins or Russian *matryoshka* dolls.

They stopped at the Barstow Creek Bar to eat bumbie burgers under banknotes from around the world.

Around Alice Springs the land was getting hillier, the trees multiplying.

A pickup truck had broken down by the side of the highway. A group of Aborigines were waving their hands at them. They'd run out of fuel and asked for a spare jerry can. Thomas opened the trunk, reluctantly, but he must have realized that here was a unique chance for a rare moment of communication. The eldest emptied the entire supply of gas into his own tank, while Thomas was shooting him with his camera. Finally, those waiting at home would have more to see than pictures of empty landscapes.

One of the women said softly: "We just got back from the bush. Got us some tucker."

She pointed at the car still greedily swallowing petrol. On the back seat lay a kangaroo, eyes closed, on a newspaper red with blood.

"Roo is good tucker. Do you want its tail? For the fuel."

Jonathan politely declined and off they went.

Thomas was mad at him: "Why did you have to tell the guy about our spare can? We need the *Benzin* ourselves. Alice Springs is another sixty kilometers, our tank's almost empty, what if we get stuck?"

At the next gas station, on the periphery of town, he paid for a whole filling. After three days on the highway, they exchanged handshakes that felt chilly in the glowing afternoon sun. Next to the dried-up bed of the Todd River, their paths readily diverged.

# Chapter 7
## *Was im Verborgenen liegt*

What lies concealed

or,

# Ellery Creek

THE HOSTEL WAS just off Todd Street. Moths were dancing frantically around the humming streetlight. The TV was on in the common room, some program about a group of people attempting to cross Lake Eyre in a canoe. The soft voice of a young woman telling the TV team: "I just need to get out there very early in the morning and sit on a rock. Then I look out over the desert and I get in touch with myself. I look at the day ahead, the one that's behind me, and then I go to my diary and write it all down."

The stars were visible through the window right next to the top bunk. Germany seemed so very far away.

Another hot cloudless day. The poinciana were in full bloom, their bright red blossoms offering ample shade in the park across from the bungalow. He walked past the basketball hoop in the yard and rang the doorbell.

It hadn't been difficult to track her. There was only one Rubinstein in the phone book. Rubinstein: it was a shiny red stone, a ruby. She had told him once that she had taken her Mom's maiden name.

No movement came from inside.

He tried several times that day, but nobody answered. He even walked by the house in the dark, but there was no light.

It was the same the next day, and the next. The neighbor, an elderly woman, was bent over the dried-up flower beds, picking things, watering the grass. It needed it badly.

"Does Alice Rubinstein live here?"

She looked up, then stretched herself, wiping her dusty hands on the apron, and walked over to the fence. Her eyes were light blue, sharp.

"May I ask who wants to know?"

"A friend," he said.

"A friend from where?"

"From Germany. We used to know each other many years ago."

She looked at him for a good while, then she said.

"Haven't seen her for days. She may have headed out to the Ranges. She goes there sometimes to be alone."

It was all right. The Ranges. East or West, he had asked. Usually, Alice would go west, she had said.

He was eager to see the area surrounding Alice Springs, but there was little point in hitchhiking out here. All roads going west sooner or later ended in sand tracks. So it was time, finally, to splurge, rent a car, and start driving through this vast landscape of red and ochre, dotted by the occasional car wreck. A land full of ghost gums, its branches standing starkly against the deep red mountain ranges, between them palm-tree-filled canyons, full of dark waters and bright blue skies.

He turned on the radio. The local station broadcast a program on Albert Namatjira, the man who had captured the essence of this landscape in his watercolors. Raised by Lower Saxon Protestant missionaries heaven-bent on converting the local Aranda: they built a church, translated the New Testament into the Aranda language, taught them German, and tried everything else possible to make them forget their traditions and ceremonies. As a youngster, Namatjira lived out bush for six months, his initiation to the land he was to paint later in life. One day two artists arrived from Melbourne, Rex Battarbee and John Gardner, and asked him to show them some scenic places they could paint, in exchange for which they taught him how to watercolor, a skill at which he soon excelled. His first exhibition in Melbourne in 1938 was a sellout. Adelaide and Sydney followed suit. Even the Queen of England admired his work. But Namatjira never felt at ease in cities, rejoicing every time he returned to the desert. One of his dreams was to buy a small farm with the riches he had earned with his paintings. For Aborigines, however, this was impossible. The land wasn't theirs to own. He couldn't even buy a house in Alice Springs. But then, in 1957, following widespread public indignation he was the first Aborigine to be awarded Australian citizenship. It meant he was now able to buy land and build a house. It also meant he could purchase alcohol. His life did not change for the better. Despite his wealth and growing reputation he and his wife lived in poverty, caught between two worlds: he was an internationally renowned celebrity and at the same time a second-class citizen. Since Aboriginal clans generally share everything they own, his family grew quickly to more than six hundred people, and he was caught again between his own people's custom of sharing with the others and the illegality of that generosity. For while he was allowed to drink, his non-citizen friends were not. When Fay Iowa, an Aboriginal woman, died after he had left a bottle of rum for members of her clan, he was sentenced to six months in prison for having supplied them with booze. Upon his release he was a broken man who could not paint anymore. And died a year later, aged fifty-seven. Heart disease was the medical diagnosis, although in his final moments Namatjira believed he was being sung to death.

He turned the radio off. Sung to death, what a strange concept it was! Did it have something to do with Chatwin's songlines? The song that kills and the songline that defines the land: once it was broken, the land too and its humans were destroyed. What traveler bound for Australia in the days just after Chatwin's death was not deeply impressed by his fictional account of aboriginal culture. Song that loses its harmony when the land undergoes even the slightest change—the construction of a road or a runway—irrevocably disfiguring the cultural memory of the dreamtime. The dreamtime . . . the genesis of Australia's indigenous people, in which their ancestors sang the world into existence: every animal, every plant, every rock, every billabong.

It was important to tread lightly out here.

Jonathan reached Ellery Creek in the late afternoon. He remembered the day Alice mentioned this billabong back in his hometown, and often he had lain awake at night trying to picture its black body. It was just a short walk from the car park to the small stretch of beach along the lake's southern curve. There was a single tent, only a few feet from the water's edge. He walked along the lake a bit, and found a secluded area where he built his own camp in the sand. Kneeling by the dark pool he touched the water. It was rather cool, its surface perfectly calm, not a ripple upon it. That strange fascination with bodies of water, lakes in particular: he had felt it since his early childhood.

"Papa, *wie tief ist dieser See?*"
"*Sehr tief, Jonathan.*"
"*Sind da Fische drin?*"
"*Natürlich.*"
"*Große Fische?*"
"*Große und kleine.*"
"*Sind die Fische gefährlich?*"

Dad had never been short of an answer, but he wasn't around for this one, which looked positively bottomless, like one of those volcanic lakes of the German Eifel Mountains that stretch as deep as the center of the earth.

*In the lagoons and billabongs along the Murray he kept looking for the bunyip. In Sydney, he had seen a picture of one, a hybrid in the shape of a horse with the teeth of a tiger, and long flowing mane. The devil-devil lay hidden in the water holes, the natives had told him, and would appear at night sometimes to drag one of their mates into the depth.*

Back at the parking lot there was a sign which mentioned the local wildlife, some of the birds found at Ellery Creek, a strange type of finch not found in most other places. But the thing that worried him was the small note saying SWIM AT YOUR OWN RISK. What did it mean? You could swim here, for sure, but if a croc got one of your legs, don't come hopping to the Australian Park Service to complain about it. Were there crocodiles this far south? He knew about the presence of salties all around the northern shores and their occasional inland migrations in search of careless campers, but surely they wouldn't have hung out around here. Sweet water crocs were a different story.

* * *

Again, he scanned the pond for a ripple on the surface, a pair of eyes emerging from its depths. Then he took off his pants and shirt, and waded in. Quickly the black water embraced him, cool to warm only at the top, his feet, however, were in its cold grasp. Rapidly, he swam across to the other side, to the small beach embedded between two imposing cliff faces. It was perfectly still here, no birds, no insects. An eerie, otherworldly place where all the clocks stop at noon. One step further and he would leave the planet, step out into a parallel universe.

Valentine's Day at Hanging Rock on his mind: the girls are forbidden any tomboy foolishness or exploration even on the lower slopes; they are being warned that the area is full of venomous snakes and poisonous ants of various species. But when they arrive, they walk further and further away from the others, observed by a young man after they cross the little creek, one after another, Miranda jumping last. *Schaut nicht die Felsenriffe, schaut nur hinauf in die Höh.* Magically they're drawn away and up through the heat-filled gum tree copse, watched by thick-lipped boulders, cave-eyed and scowling their ancient faces. And a million years old she is. Waiting a million years, just for us. From her deep shafts and crevasses unidentifiable eyes seem to be watching Miranda: she is the Botticelli angel who briefly dares to peer inside the body of the hanging rock. Venus reborn. Dropping her black shoes, her black stockings, she continues barefoot as do two of the others. Then, somewhere up there far from the group below, which appears like a cluster of ants to them, a strange thunder out of the light blue sky suddenly sends them to sleep, a Rip Van Winkle kind of sleep. Upon waking again, they're drawn higher and further, dropping their clothes, one piece after another, Cinderella stripping her shoes. Only one of them stays behind: plump little Edith; who is too slow, too scared to follow, maybe she is immune to all this romantic tomfoolery. She watches the others disappear, emitting her panic-stricken scream, that hyena scream of hysteria, putting an end to all panpipe dreams.

It all happens on the day dedicated to Juno Februata, goddess of love, and steeped in the Lupercalia, those ancient Roman festivities in honor of the wolf of foundation where eros was, and still is allowed to run wild. A heathen ritual at first, then adopted by Christianity and associated with the martyr Saint Valentine. The girls of Appleyard College, the apple orchard a symbol for the ripening of their sexuality but at the same time for control, female confinement. And then authority's deadly opposite: the Australian Venus Mountain, Miranda leading the group to their doom, shedding more than just their gloves, a place of sexual licentiousness, or rape perhaps, mysteries unsolved.

Upon descending into the shadowlands, the past is left behind, all memory has disappeared. For he led us, he said, to a joyous land, where waters gush and fruit trees grow and flowers put forth a fairer hue, and everything is strange and new. What land is Robert Browning thinking of? Jonathan remembers Alice's words from so long ago, up there on the arch of the tree looking toward the town of Hamelin, her mom's story of the Pied Piper who came out here with the children settling near Alice Springs, where the waters gush and the sun would shine, a land of joy, a land divine, all painful memories of the war left behind. Or were they not? What happens when they surface in the dead of night? Did the Romantics not know about the inevitable return of the repressed? Those early nineteenth-century poets and their insane protagonists caught between joy and terror. Like the girls of Appleyard College lured in among the rocks, unearthing what? The essence of their existence, their desires and fears, *Sehnsucht und Angst*? Forever fleeing the horizontal line, life on the plains, the plainness of life. Their liberation of sexuality from bourgeois constraints, Tieck's Christian, E. T. A. Hoffmann's Elis Fröbom, Wagner's Tannhäuser, all of them following the lure of the Venus figure. Run away, she calls to them, follow me down these rocky precipices, leave it all behind, your wives, your children, your work. The social contract. And so they do, seeking fulfillment in the mountainous world, its heights and caverns, climbing down to its interior realms, unearthing, *bergend aus dem Verborgenen*, the hidden treasures of their subconscious minds.

Sometime in the dead of night, he wakes from a noise outside the tent. Their silhouette enlarged on the canvas. One of them stops and lifts its muzzle, catches some scent but keeps wandering. But there is something else. The sound of footsteps? The nights out here play tricks on the weary traveler. Then silence. Must have been a figment of the imagination. Sleep eludes him as memories visit.

The next morning, he examines the fresh footprints in the sand, they are too small to be his own. The other tent is gone. He packs up and drives back into town.

## CHAPTER 8
### *IM INNERSTEN*
## Following the Honey-Ant Trail

"It's you again. You know, in some places this would be considered stalking."

"Sorry."

She smiled.

"So. I take it you didn't have any luck in the Ranges?"

"No."

"Try the Saturday market. She's religious about that."

Among the crowds pushing past mountains of Australiana products and assailed by the screams of the traders he walks past three T-shirts for ten dollars, past ten pairs of socks for three dollars, all the way to the farthest corners of the halls, where fruit and vegetables come in all the colors of the rainbow fish. Ten blood oranges for a dollar, who could have resisted?

He spends hours in the market halls but there is no sign of her.

Eventually the vendors start packing up.

The next day he leaves for Uluru.

The red arch is visible from a good distance. Scrambling across Uluru's dinosaur spine is tempting but he heeds the signs warning against death-bringing heat: HEAT STRESS CAN KILL. Some of those who have climbed its arching back have fallen off like Lilliputians tumbling from Gulliver's body. The Pitjantjatjara call them *minga*, ants, it's what they look like from a respectable distance, all those people pulling themselves up to the top by an iron chain.

He takes a photo, it's enough, no need to climb it, and fills up the tank of the rental car.

"Forty-five degrees," says the man at the petrol station, his left eye completely white. There is no iris, no pupil.

There is a bar, however, inside the gas station, but no draft beer.

"Just bottles, mate, but as you can see, this place is always packed."

He orders one of them.

"If I were you, mate, I wouldn't climb that mountain. Don't even take pictures."

He is pointing at his customers.

"They don't like it."

Some of his customers are smiling.

"Mount Conner, Uluru, and the Olgas are all in one line, with Uluru sticking out by three degrees. As for these fellas here, the Pitjantjatjara, Uluru's at the center of their mythology. Every rock, every tree, every crack, every hump, and every water hole has its own story. You'd better stay clear of them all. I tell everyone who comes in here, but they usually ignore me."

Leaning forward, whispering: "They take bloody photographs of rocks and cracks and say that they look like parts of the female body."

"It's Mother Earth, after all," Jonathan ventures, but they are not on the same page. The man leans in even closer.

"You know, strange things happen around Uluru. You must've heard of the mother who lost her baby, didn't you? They say a dingo took it. Not far from here. They say a dingo took it from the tent. Victim of the desert, that's what her name means: Azaria. A lot of people think it was the mother."

"What do *you* think?"

"I don't think so. Dingo's a tricky one. If you ask me, he tricked them while they weren't watching the baby."

As the haze of amber fluid took hold of Jonathan, man Dingo was emerging from the depths of time. Are you really the thief of the night they take you for, the one who steals babies under the cloak of darkness and drags them out bush, followed by the screams of the mother desperately digging around in the blankets and turning the tent upside down and inside out? Maybe she just rolled out of her blanket—such a small child, so easy to miss—but hope vanishes more and more with each searching move, panic creeping in, taking mother's breath away. Her screams into the night. She is stumbling through the darkness, searching all over, but where is she to find Azaria in the infinitude of this place, this impenetrable night? And, of course, trickster that you are, you easily get away by changing direction a few times, versatile, quick in the joints, and dragging your prey into the even darker hollow spaces of the rock.

Or did you not?

Are you like your cousin coyote who feeds on the kids of others? Are you like the Erlking of Germanic descent, that thief and murderer of children? Are you the Piper who takes children into the cave from where they never return? Are you the ogre, the demon, the witch? Are you, Dingo, swift shadow of the night, the Great Mother in the end, nurturing your own offspring, but another mother's fright? Or is one mother's neglect another mother's delight?

Sleep eludes him that night after talking to the one-eyed gas station man. His white eye kept revisiting him like a beacon in the dark. For days, his face had been hurting from sunburn. Gigantic blisters have formed under the skin, swelling his cheeks like those of a cortisone addict. How lucky, he thought, they were as kids. Their mother may have been cruel and harsh at times, but she was a lioness fiercely protective of her young. On the long drive back to Alice Springs, an old story came back to him.

As children they collected animal stickers and stuck them into ghostly white areas belonging to their rightful habitats. François was as impassioned a collector as he was in the years when they were alternating their visits between Jonathan's hometown and Le Havre. On both sides of the border, they kept begging their fathers to keep going on the animal hunt, *à la chasse des animaux*. Their dads got these stickers every time they filled up at a Shell station. He remembered the happiness he felt each time Dad came home, but especially after refilling the tank, the happiness also when François would return once again for the summer, and they traded these images. They had engaged in a sort of competition over at least three years and were anxiously looking forward to the day when either France or Germany would win the contest. Who would be able to fill all the habitats first? Who was going to be the master of all the animals on the planet? The main problem with these animals was that some of them had the tendency to turn up again and again, while others never appeared. For some strange reason, the zebra, the wildebeest, and the caribou kept visiting both France and Germany while the North American coyote, the African jackal, and the Australian dingo never did. The result was that they owned the same animals as well as a spate of duplicates which they kept for trading purposes across the border and within their communities. They kept their duplicates well hidden. But due to the many they shared, their trade had almost come to a standstill until the day when François once again appeared at his doorstep for his biannual visit.

He was radiant and the first thing he told Jonathan was that his father had chased down two new animals for him. Lo and behold, there he was releasing two dingoes into the German living room. François immediately claimed one of the elusive animals for himself, and stuck it right next to Uluru inside his album. It became slightly misplaced because his hand had been trembling from sheer joy, so that now there was a thin white line where the dingo didn't quite fill in the blank area that had been waiting for its arrival for such a long time. There was no moving this dingo into a perfect position anymore. Once a sticker got stuck it stayed stuck. François had a second dingo and Jonathan had his eye on it. He couldn't offer François any of the animals the French boy was still missing—the North American coyote, the African jackal, a spider from Nigeria, and a rare Thai monkey—simply because he didn't have them as duplicates, but he figured that five wildebeests for the dingo weren't so shabby either. But François was unyielding. He knew the value of that dingo, and although none of the collectors in Le Havre and its surrounding villages could offer him one of the animals he desired, he was hoping that someone in Germany, some other collector from the collectors' club to which Jonathan belonged, was able to enrich his collection. Jonathan gave up trying to trade with François because he knew that nothing could persuade him once he'd made up his mind.

The friendship between them might have continued

undiminished, had his mother not decided to take sides with her own flesh and blood, as well as Germany at large.

"What are you complaining about?" she said, "five wildebeests are a very generous offer for one lousy dingo."

But nothing could move François, which is why Mom wanted to force him, she wanted to force the German-French alliance which, in those years, the late 1970s, was still anything but solid.

"You'd better give him that silly dingo or you don't need to show up here anymore."

François's reaction came like a shot out of nowhere. Maybe it was so strong because his German wasn't very good, and he wanted to tell his host mother to leave him be, but for want of the right words he spontaneously came up with the next best thing someone had told him he should tell Germans whenever he wanted to be left alone by them.

With his charming accent and a faint smile spanning across his face like a butterfly François said: "*Leck misch am Arsch.*"

Mom should have thought of the strained French-German relationship, but she didn't. No kid was ever to tell her to kiss his ass without receiving the appropriate punishment. The next moment François's left cheek was adorned by five red streaks where her hand had brushed him a bit too forcefully. The imprint of her fingers left a clean white spot on one of the red long marks. Not until much later did it dawn on Jonathan that the white spot actually came from his mother's golden wedding ring.

François was positively shell-shocked. Nobody had ever laid hands on him in France, not even his parents, and he probably would have left the next day if Mom hadn't apologized to him and said: "It's OK, François. I'm truly sorry I lost my temper. I guess we'll just have to get the dingo sticker from a Shell station we haven't been to yet."

It was Saturday again, his face in the mirror peeling violently, shreds of skin hanging from his cheeks exposing pink baby skin underneath.

Back at the fruit market, the vendors look at him suspiciously. Don't touch our produce, their eyes seemed to say. He bought a dozen oranges, bright and big ones that shone with such splendor they could have given him another sunburn.

When he turned around, his heart made a jump. A woman, her head well above everyone else's was looking his way. Beyond the shadow of a doubt, it was her, her impressive height, she was even taller than he remembered her, but the same eyes, black hair and olive skin that he remembered.

She was looking his way but did not seem to recognize him.

How could she have?

He looked like a leper. People were lashing him with quick glances before turning their heads away abruptly, in disgust.

He was following her around the market halls, they were buzzing with activity around this time of day. It sounded like the humming of insects regularly interrupted by the vendors yelling out prices.

She stopped at one of the clothes stalls, fingering the T-shirts, picking up this, then that, holding one against her body, and inspecting the quality of the fabric by pulling it slightly.

Their eyes met as the plastic bag broke open, sending a dozen oranges rolling around. Falling on his knees, he started to crawl after them. It was a moment of pure and essential present, when everything stands still, past and future knocking on the door. Like a vacuum, this sudden perfect silence, no scream of marketeers, just his heart pounding in his ears. Seeking shelter under tables ripe with fruit, but no place to hide.

Her face against the light.

The sun playing with her hair, snakes of Medusa.

She stoops down to pick up one orange that has rolled to her feet, and hands it to him.

"Is it you?"

Their eyes locked together.

"Have we met?"

Her voice again, after all these years. She is searching his face, trying to remember.

"It's me. Jonathan."

"Jonathan?"

"Yes. From Bad Norndorf."

"What happened to your face?"

"Sunburn."

She smiles. Her radiant brown eyes.

"I followed your advice," he says over lunch.

"Oh, yes? What advice was that?"

"You told me once I should go to Australia because it's a healthy place."

She smiles. "Well, do you find it so?"

"I'm not so sure."

He tells her about the trip. All the people he had met. The hike on Fraser Island. Getting stranded on the road north of Mt Isa. All that German wanderlust, and yet, also about the distrust he had in hitchhiking. You never knew who would pick you up. He had been warned that people would just disappear and never be seen again.

"You're brave to be hitchhiking here. But it can be a very healthy place, too. I mean, in a spiritual sense. There was a time in my life when I needed to get away from it all. The desert was the right place to turn to. But I think I'm getting ready to leave again."

"And go where?"

"I'm not sure."

"I wouldn't mind immigrating to Australia, you know."

"What . . . leave Europe?"

"I knew a guy in Sydney who told me that if the only thing I ever achieved in life was to become an Australian citizen, it would still have been a very successful life."

"Maybe migration is preferable to immigration," she said. "Just keep going. It's what I'd like to do."

"I'm thinking of doing a loop around this place. At some point in the next few weeks my visa will run out, and I'll have to leave the country anyway. Only briefly, though. I could come back for another six months."

"Where will you go?"

"Don't know, maybe New Zealand."

She is sipping her cappuccino.

"Why did you leave Germany so suddenly back then?"

She has been looking at him all along, but now her eyes move to the jukebox next to her. She gets up, walks over, leans over the titles, and puts a coin in.

"What kind of music do you like?"

Silence spreads between them as INXS blasts forth from the speakers. *Don't ask me. Don't have to tell you. Two worlds collide. Never tear us apart.*

She sits down again. Stirs her cappuccino, stares at the brown coffee patterns in the foam.

"Let's just say, something happened that made my immediate return to Australia necessary."

Takes a sip.

"It's funny," she says, "running away from Germany is a sort of family tradition with us. My mother did it too once. Ran all the way to Australia just after the war. And now *you* have, too"

He walked her home. "Look at this," she said, kneeling in front of the flower beds in her yard. "It's a honey ant." She had picked up a small red ant on a dry leaf, a golden bubble the size of a marble attached to the rear of its tiny body. "Must have lost its clan. You can eat these, the bubble, I mean. But you need to suck the honey out very carefully, otherwise the ant dies." She put it back down. "A bit of sweetness in a land so harsh."

They hugged, briefly. There it was again, that strange intoxicating smell of hers. He knew what it was now. It had been haunting him for years, and one day he came across it, walking in an alley full of maple trees in May. It was the smell of trees with piebald trunks, maples, planes and sycamores, the juice of their bark in spring. More intense in the fall.

The next day they met again at the same place.

"You know what?" she said.

"What?"

"Do you need a travel companion? My mother wants me in Sydney. She needs to go to Germany to see her brother. And I've barely put stakes down here."

Travelling together: it was what people did around here. To feel safe. To brace the hostile elements together until solitude became preferable again.

"Yes," he said quietly. "That'd be nice."

"Let's run then."

Her eyes sparkled.

He asked her: "Do you like hitchhiking?"

"Never done it. Don't you think it's too dangerous? There are a lot of weirdos out here."

"I know. People keep telling me about the psychopath who keeps killing hitchhikers. But he operates around Sydney mostly. So, no worries. I'll protect you."

She smiled. "How would you do that? Last time it was me protecting you. Remember?"

They sat across from each other for a meal of chocolate shake and nachos with sour cream. He got up and walked over to the jukebox. There was a dead moth in it. It was trembling with each song, pushed around by the vibrations of the speaker. He threw in a coin and picked randomly.

*I want to reach out and touch the flame. I'll show you a place high on a desert plain. And when I go there, I go there with you.*

"Promise me," she said, "that we take buses too."

# Chapter 9
## *KREISLAUF*

The course of a circle, circulation, or a cyclical journey

"My soles of wind," she said. Her hiking boots were veritable seven-league boots.

In next to no time they were in Henbury. There was a camel farm on the eastern side of Stuart Highway, across from it a gas station. He asked the owner if they could pitch their tents. Jim used to be the tenant of a ranch on the road to Kings Canyon, a lucrative roadhouse on the way to paradise, he said.

"A few years ago, I had to give it all up and build a new life for me here. Me and my Dad lived there for thirty years. He discovered Kings Canyon in the early 1960s, you know, and carved a road all the way into it, making it accessible for tourism. Damn nice business, we saw it grow over the years. Unfortunately, we never owned it."

"How can anyone ever own paradise?"

"Well, my lovely lady," Jim continued. "Some rich bloke did in the end. Bought it when it was still relatively cheap. He saw right away that it was a bonanza. Hired a new tenant as soon as he bought the place. That's why we're here now."

His eyes wandered to a green sofa. There was an old man on it, fast asleep. Jim reached into a drawer and pulled out a book. "The history of our ranch." He pointed at a photo of himself as a younger man, all tanned, a broad smile on his face as he is leaning against his pickup.

"The only thing we took with us is that old truck. You must have seen it out there by the fuel pumps. It doesn't run anymore, just rots away in the sand."

His bar was filled with treasures from all over the world, the walls teeming with boxer shorts, sports badges, license plates, hundreds of banknotes.

"Nice collection," Alice said.

"We're not the only ones along Stuart Highway with such a collection. Every year there is a contest to find out who has the most beautiful bar of the Northern Territory. Daly Waters won last year. Barrow Creek has banknotes worth well over five thousand dollars. I'm sure they're going to win this year. These here are only about two thousand dollars' worth of notes, but I reckon I got a pretty good chance. It isn't just the value that leads to victory. What's important is the way you arrange things in your bar, the aesthetics so to speak, or the rareness of an object. Look at this one here, a license plate from Greenland. Must be the only one in the whole bloody country. And see that over there, it's a two-dollar note from the States, and right over here, these boxer shorts, believe it or not, but they once belonged to Kevin Keegan."

"How do you know?"

"The man himself gave them to me."

"But how can you prove that during the contest?"

"The others will believe me if I tell them. Out here a man's word of honor goes a long way, you know."

He had often wondered about the strange obsession people have with hoarding stuff. Was there a link between living out here on the desert and collecting things? Was it more than just a sense of perfectionism, a striving for completion, of acquiring something rounded and self-contained, setting borders and limits in a land as limitless as this? Or did Jim and the other outback hoarders attempt to set their collections against the harsh life out here, a piece of *Gemütlichkeit* against the inhospitality of the terrain? Were they able in this way to overcome their own isolation and distance from the rest of the world by opening small glimpses to other parts of the world, while at the same time creating a sense of community through their contests? Or were they modern-day nomads, hunters, and gatherers? Was the obsession to collect in the end an atavistic nomadic instinct to own something in a land that cannot be owned?

"You can't rule this land," Jim resumed. "All you can do is find a niche where you can survive. You just gotta be humble. Humility: that's what I've learned out here. You just gotta be humble."

The flies were up a long time before them. Alice stepped out of the shower and they immediately descended upon her, competing with the sun for the drops on her skin. They hitched their first ride with an Aborigine who had driven through the night.

"Where you going?" he asked.

"Coober Pedy."

"Shoulda thought so. Everyone's goin' to Coober Pedy. To look for opals, or to Uluru. To climb the rock."

"I was there many times," said Alice. "and never climbed it. And we aren't interested in opals."

"You're exceptional," he said softly.

"She is," said Jonathan.

The man smiled.

"Most people coming out here go either deep into the earth or high into the sky. I prefer horizons. Speaking of which," he turned around, "do you mind taking the wheel while I stretch out in the back. I'm as tired as a dog. Already nodded off twice. Wake me in Erldunda, would you."

He stretched out on the loading space of his pickup.

They woke him in Erldunda, gave him back his truck, and with a wave he disappeared west down Lasseter Highway.

Brian was on his way from Cairns to Perth and had made it this far in two days. Cannonballing, he called it.

Almost with a sense of pride, Brian said: "I know nothing about other countries. But I know Australia like the back of me hand."

He was driving in search of work, didn't want to wait until work came to him but kept chasing it around the continent.

Brian also suffered from a pigment disorder on his face. His skin was red and white, piebald lobster red and white like an albino cow with partial sunburn. He kept joking about Alice's long legs, as she had to sit sideways in the back, but he was obviously quite attracted to her.

"You're not a seppo, pretty lady, right?"

She gave him a puzzled look.

"And your friend here, where is he from? Is he a seppo?"

"What do you mean?" she asked him.

"Never heard of it? Aussie rhyming slang. Short for *septic tank*, which rhymes on yank. Seppoes are all a bit shitbrained."

He got all excited about his joke, which turned the red spots on his face an even deeper red, while the white ones stood out as ghostly as a gum tree on red sand.

"Gosh, seppoes are so gullible. I once went camping to Ayers with my ex-wife. We met a whole group of them. They asked us if it was safe to climb to the top. Sure it's safe I told them, there's an iron chain, takes you right up. Almost like a lift. Like a tow rope at one them ski resorts, you just hold on to it, and up you go. No worries, and when you get to the top there's a coke machine, and you know what? They actually believed me. Fair dinkum. I still hear one of them like it was yesterday. He screams: 'Hey Harry! Did ya hearr what this guy said. Therre's a coke machine at the top.'"

They were both quiet.

"Have you been up there? No? Why not? Sacred mountain? Don't make me laugh. If you ask me, it's the best bloody source of income in the whole bloody Northern Territory."

He snorted, baring yellow teeth.

"Do you think we should leave the rock to the Aborigines? And tell the tourists to go home? Let me tell ya: that would be a bad mistake."

He could sense Alice's discomfort. They both kept quiet. There was no getting through there. People with firm opinions, it was impossible to sway them.

"What about you, pretty lady? Who are your people? You partly Aborigine? You're an Aussie girl, right?"

"Depends how you define an Aussie girl. My mother is German, my father from Tahiti. But I grew up in Australia."

He dropped them off outside Coober Pedy. Politely, they thanked him and said their goodbyes.

After a few steps Alice broke the silence.

"I wonder what it is that makes them think they're so superior? Europeans, I mean. They have spread disease and alcoholism among people who never knew about ulcers, obesity, or high blood pressure until the whites arrived. Why would they be more civilized than the indigenous who recognize the cosmic will in all human beings, animals, plants, and even rocks."

They kept walking down the dusty road.

"The Romantics did."

She looked at him inquisitively.

"I mean, the Romantics saw a deeper animation in rocks and mountains. Coleridge, Tieck, Thoreau. Yet their affinity with the natural world was fragile. It was the beginning of capitalism, industrialization, and utilitarian thinking. The idea of exploiting nature had already been born. The bourgeois age: it meant exploiting the peaks and summits for recreation, and drilling into the earth, mining its hidden treasures."

He was quickly warming up to one of his favorite topics.

"Take Heinrich Heine, for example. He was a political writer exiled from Germany to cosmopolitan Paris, but his views were rooted in German romanticism. He wrote a book about the Harz Mountains, they're close to where I grew up. Heine verbally attacks the hikers on the Brocken peak, a mountain steeped in myths about the witches' Sabbath. The famous Walpurgis Night is said to take place there every midsummer. When Heine reaches the top he gets very impatient with some of his fellow citizens, the philistines as he calls them, who praise the sunset and think that nature puts on this spectacle solely for their amusement. In his eyes the philistines just exploit nature.

Or take Ludwig Tieck, you might have heard of him. He's one of my favorites. The one who wrote *Puss in Boots*, you know? Tieck has a character in one of his stories, *The Rune Mountain*, who gives up his Christian, small-town life, family and friends, and is driven into wilderness, where he has a vision of the woman of his dreams, a kind of mythical figure. She can be seen as Mother Nature, both nurturing but also exploited, violated in a way, by mankind in the age of industrialization. The character's final descent into the interior of the mountain landscape, into their mines, is highly eroticized through this figure. But by stripping the ground of its treasures, pebbles, and gemstones, he himself partakes of the spirit of capitalist exploitation while running away from it at the same time. She's a strange figure really, his titanic mountain queen, promising both joy and terror, beauty and ugliness. While beautiful one moment, as soon as she turns her back on him all he can see is the dead bark of a giant tree."

He had worked up quite a sweat. Did she think he was a complete geek? All that book knowledge.

Alice looked at him pensively. How pretty she was. Those fine brows arching over her dark soulful eyes, her Roman nose and sensual mouth. But she was rather pale, something seemed to weigh on her mind.

"Wow. Where's all this coming from? Looks like you really know your literature."

"I've studied it for years. German lit, myth, folklore. I've always been fascinated by these stories. Do you remember when you talked about the Pied Piper back then on top of our tree? You know, when you told me about your mother and the children of Hamelin walking all the way through the center of the earth until they came out again over here in Central Australia."

"Ah, that," she smiled. "Yes, I remember. But what about those children in the legend, disappearing in the mountain. How do you interpret that?"

"Well," he continued in his professorial way to impress her, "to some he was a demagogue leading Hamelin's youth away from the bourgeois world of its citizens. To others, he was a recruiter for the purpose of war or for resettlement in Eastern Europe. According to several versions, the children disappeared in the mountains near Hamelin but reappeared in Transylvania. Writers like Bertolt Brecht and Günter Grass have seen Adolf Hitler as a historical embodiment of the medieval piper, his extermination of rats and abduction of children signifying the extermination of undesirables and abduction of a whole people. But possibly in the end, the rat-catcher of Hamelin was no other than a serial killer, a psychopath and pederast, who sometime in the thirteenth century spirited away 130 children and used them in unspeakable ways."

Alice had become even more serious.

"I wonder if the mountain entrance of the legend was a real place. I've often asked myself if the mineshaft my mother survived in during the war years was that very same place."

"She survived in a mineshaft?"

She nodded.

"Where is it?"

"It's close to where you grew up. Those mountains to the south of your hometown Bad Norndorf. You remember the view from that arching tree where you took me. The day that boy attacked us. Those hills. We talked about them. Remember? You said they were full of mines, with some leading through the mountains and that some had an exit. I assume it was one of them."

"How could she survive in there? For how long?"

"I don't know. A long time, I reckon. She never talks about it. All I know is that her brother, Uncle Wolfram, took her there so she'd be safe. A friend of his, Hermann, helped her with food and blankets. I think he hid her at his house too. It wasn't pretty when she came out at the end of the war. All she saw was devastation. Corpses sitting in their cars. The hatred on the faces of British soldiers. There was pillaging everywhere. Rape."

"What does your mother do now?"

"She's a historian at the University of Sydney. She specializes in the history of Germans migrating to Australia. Piecing the past together, I suppose. Her own past as well."

"And your father?"

"He's back in Tahiti. Happily oblivious to us, painting South Sea life."

"Sounds like a book by Somerset Maugham."

"Yeah, I know. *The Moon and Sixpence*."

They had entered Coober Pedy.

"I need a drink," she said, breaking the silence. Large beads of sweat had formed on her forehead.

It was a good idea. They were both parched. It was infernally hot.

"These people live underground, you know."

"Another set of modern-day Romantics, I'd say."

Like moles the Coober Pedians had thrown up hundreds of little white hills pockmarking the earth's surface all around town. Digging for opals. Underground, the heart was able to find everything it desired: shops, banks, even churches. But they got there during the day, and the streets of Coober Pedy were swept empty.

"Let's keep going," Alice said. "This place gives me the creeps."

There was no immediate getting out of town, so they went to the pub. It was the usual smell of sweat and spilled beer. The room was filled with coarse humanity, some of them fighting, and nowhere else so far had he seen the local population in a more desolate state. Everyone seemed to have gone mental with digging for unearthed treasures.

And here now all of a sudden, right in the middle of them, stood Alice, their Venus figure.

The room went silent when they walked in.

When he ordered two ginger beers, the barkeeper's face assumed an expression of irritation. For a moment it wasn't clear whether he was going to serve them at all. Surprisingly, though, he did.

The next day they dragged their packs back to Stuart Highway, where they greased their thumbs with high protection sunscreen. There was plenty of traffic, but it was the usual story. Nobody stopped.

He read to her from Hesse's *Siddhartha*. His soul tasting the bleak euphoria of the cyclical journey. Trying to flee the Self a thousand times, lingering in nothingness, in the animal, in stone, but his return was unavoidable.

After three hours they walked back into town. Maybe there was a bus going south.

It turned out all buses were booked because of the holidays.

They might be able to get stand-by tickets, they were told. If they were lucky. But not until three in the morning. It was a twelve-hour wait.

After the first three hours a man came over: Jack from Monterey, California, around 40, a German teacher for the US Army.

"You gotta be from the States or Canada."

It was his accent again. Jonathan was proud of it. He was a human chameleon, like Woody Allen's Leonard Zelig. Like him, he adapted quickly to whoever he talked to in terms of accent and sometimes even gestures. Some might have called it a weakness; he called it talent. Of course, he was flattered that the man from California didn't think he was German. How very German of him, that blend of self-hatred and perfectionism, the perfect breeding ground for incorrigibility.

He finally admitted to Monterey Jack that he was from Germany.

"Oh yeah? Whereabouts?"

"Near the Bavarian Alps."

There was no point in telling him about the North German spa town. He wouldn't have heard of it. Americans knew Munich, maybe Frankfurt, and they knew Berlin. Everything else was terra incognita to them. If you said Hanover or Bremen, they would ask you if it was in the West or the East.

"Oh yeah? I've lived in Bad Tölz for years."

Bad Tölz: it was another spa town, much nicer than the one he had grown up in, thanks to Bavarian-style *Gemütlichkeit* and a US army base. Since Jack was a teacher, Jonathan thought it was a good idea to tell him about his Master's degree. He added that he would one day like to teach literature.

But his education seemed to offend the man from Monterey:

"Oh yeah? I've seen a lotta teachers in my days—people with no fancy-schmancy degrees who teach a lot better than people who've spent years at some university."

Jack sized him up:

"I hate people like you."

Was he yet another psychopath pursuing his solitary songline? Had the heat gotten to him?

"Why's that? Why do you hate people like me?"

"Just being facetious. People like you who speak perfect English and live in one of the most livable places in the world."

"Although nothing really beats California," he added.

"My German is perfect," said Jack, "But I refuse to ever speak it outside the classroom. How come your English is so good?"

So Jonathan told him that for the longest time it had been one of his greatest aspirations in life to join the KGB. This triggered a volley of abuse directed, however, primarily at Jack's ex-wife. Jack kept accusing her of being one of the worst communists he had ever met, pronouncing the word like 'cummunist' and making a face as if it were the plague. Repeatedly he was wiping his greasy hand on his T-shirt, which announced in large letters that America would be a tobacco-free society by the year 2000.

He kept cutting thick slices from a Hungarian Pick salami.

Jonathan asked him if he'd ever been to Hungary, but Jack didn't want to hear about Hungary. They were Cummunists too.

"Did you serve in the German Army?"

"No."

"How come? Don't you guys all have to join for two years?"

It was a touchy topic. The doctors had declared him *untauglich*, unfit, literally without value. The verdict had been *Kreislaufschwäche*, a weakness of the circulation system, one of those imaginary German afflictions.

But Jack didn't need to know all this. So instead of telling him about his medical history, Jonathan dished up the usual little story about how he moved to West Berlin just in time before the army could lay their claws on him. West Berlin was an army-free zone in the days of the Cold War. The man from Monterey didn't want to know about army-free zones, maybe because they couldn't be compartmentalized into either Capitalism or Cummunism, so the two of them fell silent for a while.

He reached for the diary jotting down the dialogues that had just passed between them. Suspiciously, Jack glanced at his writing and said: "Your handwriting is like that of a ductor." Proudly he added: "I never write down anything besides the names of the places I go through."

In the evening hours, he called his parents, while Alice was trying to secure two plastic chairs next to a gas pump.

Dad wasn't feeling well. His heart was giving him problems. But he didn't complain. Life was good. Had been very good to him. It was his father on the phone, but Jonathan could barely hear him. Mom was yelling in the background. She avoided coming to the phone and talking to him directly but at the same time kept talking in the background over everything his father was trying to say, so after a while Dad just stopped talking altogether. Too expensive, was all Jonathan heard him say still. And: Calling from Australia.

It was rather typical: his parents were always worried about phone charges. So they hung up.

Chewing ice cubes from a two-liter bag momentarily soothed the pain of lips ravaged by the hot wind and cracked so badly that the blood kept seeping out of them.

"Look how scarred the land is around here." Alice's eyes were holding the sunset. "By wounding the earth humanity wounds itself. And hurting the land is like hurting the body. I saw you reading Bruce Chatwin's *Songlines* yesterday. I love his concept of lending a stretch of land to others through song, rather than owning the land. You can never own the land, the Aboriginals know that. It's the same with the human body: it should never be owned by others."

"You mean you can just lend out your body to someone? Lend it out through song? And that lending then is love?"

She nodded.

"And when someone insists on owning your body?"

She looked at him long and hard for a moment. Then she pulled Chatwin's book from his pack. "I'm somewhat skeptical though about some of his theories. Especially all that stuff about peaceful nomads."

She was leafing through the book.

"It's interesting also what he says about Carl Strehlow's writings about the Aranda tribe. Strehlow—he was a compatriot of yours. But he grew up here in Australia, in Hermannsburg, where his father ran a Lutheran mission. He spoke perfect Aranda and was the first one to acknowledge that the intellect of the indigenous people was in no way different from that of the Europeans. He recognized this a long time before Claude Lévi-Strauss. Did you know that there used to be two completely different ethnic groups among the Aranda, a nomadic one and a sedentary one? The sedentary tribe used to think of itself as the nobler race. They thought they were a pure race. Their people were extremely tall and proud, they loved war and were inflexible in their customs and rituals, they had extremely violent initiation rites and apparently they must have been extremely serious and lacking in humor."

"Are you sure they were Aranda people and not Germans?"

She smiled. "Why? Don't you like the Germans? C'mon, they're your people. Well, the other group, the nomads among the Aranda of the western deserts were short, but they were extremely open-minded to the customs of other people. They roamed across the land, which they loved deeply and would never have called their own. They were people who hadn't forgotten how to laugh, unlike their brothers just north of here."

At sundown they lost the two chairs. Underground, there was a hostel where they tried to temporarily store their packs. A woman with an excessively foul temper, the hostel manager, started yelling at them when they told her they were going for one last drink in Coober Pedy.

"That bus driver won't take you if you come back here drunk."

What business was it of hers? Reading his thoughts she snapped:

"If you want me to look after your packs, you should at least have the courtesy of heeding my advice."

Toward ten, they returned from the pub and lay down on the veranda of a motel to find some sleep but were driven away by the manager. There was not a patch of grass to bed one's head, no park in the entire town. Just the dust outside the hostel where resting their heads on the packs suddenly seemed like a great luxury.

Two Europeans passed by, Dutch or Swedish, both very drunk: "You American? Hey man, I wouldn't live there. No culture. Only McDonald's."

Finally, they managed to close their eyes for a few hours. At four in the morning they got two seats on the bus to Adelaide. The eternal tock-plock of the animals dying on the roo bar, that metal frame at the front of most outback vehicles, sent Alice into deep oblivion long before him, her head sinking upon his.

# CHAPTER 10
## *MÜNDUNGEN*

### Estuaries

"MOM'S DONE A lot of research on the German settlers in this area. I remember, she used to tell me about a German postman out here. His name was Tom Kruse, a sort of outback legend, operating the Birdsville Track. That's a very lonely unpaved road out there, which loses itself somewhere in the interior. Since the 1930s that guy was delivering mail to the most remote areas, fighting with sand storms and flashfloods, and doing the same route year after year, thousands of miles just in this part of the world."

There were stunning views of the Flinders Ranges in the distance.

"It makes me wonder sometimes," she continued, "how often Kruse traveled the circumference of the globe without actually seeing anything other than northern South Australia. I guess, in the end that poses the question if one really needs to travel far to see the world. Or is the world also contained in a small segment of it?"

"Maybe," he said, "there are only two ways of traveling: flat-map and deep-map travel. Deep-map travel is when you retrace your steps over and over in a small segment of the world until you know it in all its nuances and are acquainted with everyone's life in it. I suppose that kind of travel fills you with a deep sense of home.

"And flat-map travel?"

"It's those who run around the whole globe. Who try to see everything."

She looked at him and said: "You mean, like Chatwin?"

"Yeah, or Friedrich Gerstäcker."

"Who's he?"

"He was a German travel writer and adventurer whose Australian journey I've been reading on this trip."

"So what's preferable in the end, deep-map or flat-map travel?"

"Hard to say. One has more variety, the other possibly more intensity. Maybe it's best to have a bit of both," he said. "I think Gerstäcker actually had both. He traveled all over the planet while also obtaining a deep sense of home in the woods of Arkansas."

Then there was Hans Heysen, she said, another German drawn to the Flinders Ranges, he would have been a deep-map-kind-of-guy, who devoted a lot of attention to detail, mostly to gum trees. He loved the large trees lining the dried-out riverbeds around here, their defiant strength. To him they embodied the spirit of perseverance of the early settlers, his own too in following his calling as a painter, a profession that made it almost impossible to provide for his wife and their eight children. All those landscape painters, she said, the Namatjiras and Heysens in this country, they touched the land ever so gently, with their brushes, their watercolors and oils. They spent hours, days, a lifetime caressing the landscapes with their eyes while seated on tiny stools in the heat with millions of flies buzzing around their heads.

"Heysen," she said, "was one of the many German-Australians during the First World War who fell victim to the surges of hatred and xenophobia that swept across South Australia with devastating consequences for the German settlers. This happened especially after Gallipoli and the sinking of the Lusitana. The German immigrants here were persecuted primarily for their lifestyle and their Lutheran German-speaking schools. Most of them were shut down. It was forbidden to the Germans to hold their services, their clubs were closed, their newspapers suppressed."

Her mother, she said, had been working on German immigration and settlement in Australia for years. The first Germans, Alice told him, had come here in the thirties and forties of the nineteenth century in search of religious freedom and economic advantages. They arrived in Port Adelaide, then called Port Misery, hoping for a better quality of life than their home country could afford them. The first years were anything but easy for these families. Food was scarce and many of them starved to death. Gradually, thanks to their Protestant work ethic and wholesome kangaroo meat, they got back on their feet, however, and founded settlements such as Hahndorf, Klemzig, Rosenthal, Hoffnungsthal, Lobethal and Langmeil, all of them small towns near Adelaide.

Discipline and hard work were the two main virtues by which the Germans excelled as pioneers and earned their neighbours' respect, although their Lutheran schools formed enclaves within a predominantly Anglo-Saxon culture. These Germans believed firmly that the Lutheran faith could only be taught through the German language. An education without this faith was unthinkable to them, since it taught their children such essential values as discipline, loyalty toward their families, a simple way of life, and deep piousness.

Following the dissolution of their elementary schools in 1917 these communities lost the basis of their existence. The Protestant Church tried as hard as possible to convince the Australian government that the church's insistence on a German education was in no way linked to Germany's imperialist goals, but parliamentarians like John Verran pursued ruthless anti-German policies suggesting that the German settlers be deprived of all their rights.

Verran's insistence that all Germans be kicked out of the country was supported by newspapers like the patriotic *The Mail* from Adelaide according to which all Germans in Australia were allies of the emperor, Kaiser Wilhelm. Violent transgressions toward the Germans were a consequence of this fuelling of hate. German houses were pillaged and Lutheran churches burnt to the ground.

"There were even concentration camps for Germans," she said, "where families lived in squalid conditions until they were released again at the end of the war."

The South Australian Lutherans did little to defend themselves, but kept reiterating that since the early days of their settlement they had expressed their loyalty to the British crown and the Australian government. And that they had prayed for both but never for the German government.

At Sellicks Beach just south of Adelaide, they caught a ride with an eccentric lady with untamable hair. The road wound through golden prairie hills studded here and there by tall solitary trees. Her face was as furrowed as the Ganges delta. She was on her way back to Melbourne from Western Australia, WA as she called it, where she had been traveling for a year.

"That's the best place on Earth," she insisted, "it's totally wild, the beaches are hundreds of kilometers long with nobody on them. Sand as white as snow, the sea bluer than the Mediterranean."

"Have you seen the Mediterranean?"

"I have. Been up and down Europe. Didn't like it. The people there are prisoners of their own wealth. There's a sort of mindless materialism in Europe. Greece was OK."

Every time her VW bus leaned into a curve, her countless treasures from the beaches of WA—sun-bleached seashells, dried seaweed, even a few fleshless fish heads—went traveling over her dashboard.

She drove as far as Goolwa.

In the next car that stopped was Jim Jarvis, almost sixty and not a believer in overdressing. He shook hands solemnly for what seemed like an eternity, first with Alice, looking up at her in awe, then with him. Having spent thirty years in the army, he said, he was now a free spirit.

"Come to my house. Meet my people."

His house was right across from the isolated campground and his people were all sitting round the TV.

"What do you want to drink? The choice is milk or rain water." He poured them some rain water. "Why don't you look at the Coorong?"

"What's the Coorong?" asked Jonathan.

Jim said it was a large swamp near the estuary. Every now and then, there were some who attempted to cross it. They spent hours leaning over his topographic maps. Jim knew every dune, every shallow spot in the river.

"You gotta watch out right here. Quicksand. And right here I saw a brown snake the other day. You know, one bite and you hear the angels sing."

Jim told them about one of the early explorers who crossed the estuary at low tide.

"When he got to the other side he was speared to death. What would *you* do if someone tried to break into your house?"

He gave them the topo maps as a present and kissed Alice goodbye while she was still sitting. Turning to Jonathan he said: "She's Miss Right, you know. Bit tall maybe, but I should know. I've met a lot of she-devils in my time."

He kissed her again.

"I'd kiss you too," he said to Jonathan, "if you weren't so bearded."

*As he was walking west, he noticed how the landscape changed from a dull, flat monotony to a sudden rise of high limestone cliffs flanking the river. The soil was a gray heavy loam that stuck to his feet. He repeatedly had to use his bowie knife to scrape the thick crust off his heels. Walking along, he wondered about the consummate ignorance of the English settlers in dealing with the indigenous tribes they encountered. The English, he thought, were in fact the most singular people in the world in their treatment of foreign languages. They travel, he wrote in his diary, through the whole known and unknown world without thinking it necessary—with exceptions, of course—to ever learn any language but their own. He thought of himself as a great deal more enlightened than this. He was surprised that the English settlers he came across in Southern Australia took no greater interest in the local people with whom they were in constant contact, while the latter were obliged to learn English if they wanted any conversation at all. His own interest in the indigenous led him so far even as to visit their burial grounds. It was a bad mistake, as they hated nothing more than a white man profaning the graves of their dead.*

*It was after visiting their tombs that he could not help but feel that he was being followed. For two full days, he sensed the presence of someone behind him. Whenever he stopped and looked around it seemed as if some dark shadow flashed across the small trek he had carved through the bush, no farther away than about two hundred yards behind him. His heart was beating faster when he asked himself what business anyone could have following him; whoever they were they were most certainly bent on mischief. And although he had made it his rule not to shed human blood, nor hurt a native if he could help it, he was fully determined not to let them get any advantage over him. He felt curious to know what they would do as soon as they discovered him watching them.*

*At the end of the second day of being followed, as the afternoon light was getting more and more golden, he was suddenly startled by a small flock of black cockatoos that came rushing over the bushes, alighting on the trees above him. It had been his experience that Australian birds were not as shy and fidgety as European ones. Even in Sydney, he had been able to easily walk past a bird less than a few feet away from him without it running or flying away. But something seemed to have disturbed these black cockatoos, for they dispersed as quickly as they had come, screaming and darting off in every direction. Lowering his face back down from the sky thus set in motion by hundreds of black darting shadows he caught the last of two dark figures gliding across the small trail only a hundred yards away from him.*

*He was tired of being chased like a wild animal.*

*He didn't think much about the consequences but raised his gun and released a load after them, just as they disappeared into the bush. At the same moment, scarcely leaving him time to jump out of the way, he saw something fly at him. It was one of their long spears approaching in a high arc. He followed the javelin with his eyes, ready to dodge it, but was happy to see that it got stuck in the sand just behind him. Walking in the direction whence the weapon had emerged, he could not discover the hand that had thrown it, nor did he find any blood in the tracks of the two shadows he had shot at. He was hoping that they were more frightened than hurt. Fortunately, he writes, from that minute on they gave up the chase.*

Below them the sea is crashing onto the beach. Dense forested hills on their left. Lorikeets, white yellow-crowned cockatoos, and gray-pink galahs shoot up from the thick tangle of eucalypts, fluttering and screeching into the rich blue coastal sky. Accompanied by the constant whirring of the insect world. Naked gum trees are sloughing off their bark like snake skin, forming juiceless heaps on the sun-flooded path leading to the beach.

At the campground kiosk they order hamburgers with the works. A fried egg, pineapple ring, red beet, bacon, ketchup, lettuce leaf, and the obligatory beef patty—wolf it all down before the sauce runs from the double-decker. It is early in the afternoon, and there are only a few families with their kids, dogs, towels, and picnic baskets. The kids are playing in a shallow pool cut off from the sea. The beach lies protected between two high cliffs hollowed by the ocean. With their myriads of holes and caves, the porous sandstone looks like an aged Emmental cheese.

Terrified by their approach, countless glassy-eyed, purple-pincered crabs take flight in the direction of the waves furiously pounding the sand. Waves either rolling over and suffocating within themselves or stretching out over the long beach reaching for ever more dry sand, flattening wind-whipped ribs before being reclaimed by the sea.

Leaving behind some of her treasures and a thin wet film.

The sun and salt on their skin.

Smell of seaweed.

Far out, where the sea is almost black and the highest breakers are tossing their warrior manes, some surfers brave the elements in their black orange suits. Lying on their boards, they're paddling as close to the wave's crown as possible before springing into a stand just before the wave breaks. Riding down with it they use the momentum of their descent to quickly bring their boards around. Then they climb back up to the top again where they perform a 180-degree gyration before schussing into the abyss. The gyrations send some of them tumbling into the sea, their boards shooting elsewhere so that the surfers have to start swimming for them.

He wonders why they aren't haunted by the terror of these waters, the Great White who might mistake them for seals. If they're lucky, their legs will remain unscathed and only a piece of the surfboard will be eaten.

Where the sand has been hardened by the sea, where bare feet tread firm and cool, two men are running back and forth brandishing a string pulled tight by a slight silver weight at its end.

"Why are you dragging a dead fish along the beach?" Alice asks them.

"We're catching lug worms," says one of them, his face frightfully red. Huge pustules had formed on his purple nose, his eyes shifty, his hands twitching nervously.

"Catching worms with fish? I would have thought it's the other way around."

"Catching worms with fish, then catching fish again with

worms," he says.

The man's nose is mesmerizing. It makes Jonathan recall a picture in the National Geographic of an Australian whose nose was completely gone, in its place a plastic prosthesis and behind it a gaping hole, just like one of the cavities in the cliffs behind them.

"Those worms are deep down in the sand. They're attracted by the smell of the rotting fish. When they come up and stick their heads out, I grab them by the neck with these pincers here and pull 'em out. Some of them are up to seven feet long."

His pincers drive furiously into several spots in the sand, biting around for worm neck.

"Shit," he screams, "didn't get it. Won't show his face again for a long time, that one. He knows I'm after him."

Jonathan unpacked the picnic: bread, Philadelphia Cream Cheese, tomatoes, a bottle of red, and a few cans of Bacardi Cola Mix.

His eyes brush her swimsuit. Magnetized by her lips, the pearl white of her perfect teeth, animated by the smell of the ocean and the nearby eucalyptus trees, intoxicated by the thunder of the breakers and the beauty of the land around them and encouraged by the certainty that now, finally, they were alone on the beach, he is aching to touch her.

At that moment something wet touches his back.

What do we have here?

A blue dog with intelligent eyes. A Blue Heeler. He is jumping around on the beach, rolling over, barking. Runs between them, playful, leaning against him. Alice is patting him. "I love dogs. Don't you think that they might be trapped people?"

Jonathan jumps up, runs over to the wet sand for a cartwheel and two back-hand springs.

Alice in awe: "I didn't know you were a gymnast."

More and more, the color of the sky is adopting the same hue as the wine until night throws its cloak around them. Except for a thin white fringe at their feet the thundering waves have slipped under a mask of invisibility.

Some voices came from the other side of the dunes. Home had caught up with him.

"Boy, what a nice beach. Let's stay here. See, there are two tents over there already. What did you say? You don't want to go swimming here? Why not? We can even be completely naked here. What did you say? Sharks?! Don't be ridiculous. We won't go in very far and nothing will happen. Let's pitch the tent, and then we'll see."

Old faithful came to visit, claustrophobia—it had never let him down. His rising blood pressure provided him with the necessary energy to move the tents away.

"What's wrong?" Alice was following him.

"Germans. They're everywhere."

The disgust in his voice made her laugh. "No worries. If you're scared of them why don't you come into my tent tonight?"

*The morning he arrived in the Adelaide district, a single black swan came over the hills and alighted in a little channel formed by the rain water. Such a bird must not have been seen in these parts for many years, he thought, raised his rifle, and shot it. It had been a rough march that morning; plenty of rain and wind, the latter driving against him, particularly when he reached the tops of some of the naked and round ridges. He had to lean forward with his full body to resist its force. The vegetation here was all gum trees and good grass. Just before noon, he reached the first fences, the first plowed land he had seen for many weeks, and over there on the low hill, where the little straw thatched house was standing, he saw a man plowing with his six oxen, a woman leading them. He was more than a thousand yards distant, but he could have sworn that that man was German.*

*And he was right. He was from North Germany. Invited into his cottage Gerstäcker had to step to the window once or twice so that his old friends, the gum trees, would convince him that he was actually in Australia. Inside the house, his hosts had been able to transplant everything from their former home in Germany to this far-off and exotic land, including the smell. Not only their clothes were the same, but the tables and chairs, stoves, the glass panes in the window, the nails in the walls, the kettles, the pans and pannikins, ay, even the earthen plates and dishes with verses of Scripture written upon them. If they had taken out one of these rooms back home, packed it up carefully in cotton, and planted it again in the New World, they could not have preserved it better. And a most pleasant feeling it was for him, so far from home, to hear his mother tongue again. A tear or two ran down his cheek upon hearing it, thinking but briefly of the wife he'd left behind.*

It was near dark. The waves kept breaking steadily, sounding out his compatriots. He could smell the sea, the eucalypt and sycamore trees. Lying in a tent with Alice, with only the thin canvas-like skin between them and the untamed nature all around them, he felt strangely sheltered and vulnerable at the same time. But it was a deep feeling of happiness—of having arrived where he wanted to be.

He listened to her breathing. There was a strangely expectant silence between them, as if they were both waiting for the other one to say something first.

"Jonathan?!"

"Yes?"

"You remember when we kissed in Germany?"

"It was the night before you left."

"Did you enjoy it?"

His heart gave a little jump.

"Yes. Very."

"So did I."

Her T-shirt depicted the design of a koala done in quick brush strokes. He touched her hand and brought it toward his mouth, kissing it gently. She pulled him toward herself.

Her hot breath. He is surprised how fast her mouth yields to his response, her tongue coming right toward him. She slips off his T-shirt. Then takes off the Koala. The smell of sycamore is becoming more and more intense, wrapping up the sea. Her rosettes budding, his erection throbbing. Her lips full and soft, he keeps sinking deeper and deeper into them. His loins fizzing, he can't, can't control, there they are again, those cheeky rabbits twitching in quick succession. Surfacing, the surf back within earshot, she says:

"What's wrong?"

"It's nothing."

"Is it my size?"

Funny, shouldn't the guy be asking that?

"I'm sorry," he whispers. Those Germans next door didn't need to hear them. "Much too quick."

Her giggle. "No worries. There's always a next time."

The Germans had left early. There was no one on the beach. The sun was already intensely hot, so they stripped completely naked and ran down into the ocean, swimming beyond the waves to where it got deep quickly.

"Can you still stand here?"

"Sure." She smiled and came up to him hugging him around the neck. They kissed, her warm breath under his nose, the salt water mixing with saliva. He licked her face, she giggled, licking him all over.

"Are there sharks around here?"

"Sure." She laughed. "They're everywhere."

They walked back to where he could stand, the water was up to his chin.

"Here, let me help you." She was holding him with her left arm round his back, her right one under his thighs, his right arm slung around her neck. He felt almost completely safe from the sharks. "Look what's surfacing here," she said, "looks like someone is growing a dorsal fin."

"Let's go back to the beach."

Stretching out in the flat sand smoothed over by the stretching surf, they are kissing again. She rolls him off her, her on top now, pinning him down, her sheer physical power over his body. She pushes him down a bit, buries his face between her breasts, her midst receiving him warm and moist, waves pounding away, licking the sand from their bodies.

## CHAPTER 11
### *BRÜCKENBÖGEN*

The arches of bridges

THEY GOT PICKED up by a married couple, originally from Poland, who had emigrated to Australia twenty-seven years earlier. Warm people. "Have you seen the estuary?" the woman asked. "It's beautiful out there. It's like Hela Peninsula in northern Poland." The estuary was a strange place. Between two sandbanks the languid, wide river was stemming its body against the wild phalanxes of the Antarctic Ocean. How on earth did this river manage to flow into the sea? How could it overcome such massive resistance? But the two managed to merge somehow, mixing sweet and salty, brown and bottle green. The river laughed and gazed at them with a thousand eyes.

The two Poles were talking nonstop. They wanted to give them money, he wasn't sure why, maybe it was because they looked so disheveled. He was thinking about taking it for a moment, but politely, Alice declined. The Polish woman took it the wrong way. Her husband kept insisting: "Just take it. Come on. Money goes, money comes."

Their next lift was with a madman: about sixteen, he opened his trunk with a screwdriver, threw in their bags, and off he shot.

"Where you going?"

"Nowhere. Just down the road. Givin' the car a good thrashing."

The kid came down hard on the accelerator and took off for a suicidal passing maneuver. The engine almost exploded.

"Takin' the car out, eh?"

"Yeah. Blowin' the cobwebs out of the engine."

He loved maltreating the gear shaft. Saw himself on some sort of speedway.

"Does the seat belt work?"

"Wouldn't know."

Alice asked: "Is Warrnambool a pretty big town?"

They were somewhere between Portland and Warrnambool, about 50 kilometers apart from one another. He lived in Portland and said: "Never heard of it."

Jonathan asked him what the Twelve Apostles were like.

"No idea. Never been out there."

The landscape had to be absolutely lovely, Jonathan assumed. It passed by in a blur. "I think we're going for a walk," he ventured a bit meekly.

The kid immediately switched down: "I'm droppin' youse off."

Then he made a U-turn and his engine howled a farewell.

They had only traveled three kilometers down the road. Their next ride was with an old man who was stone deaf but got them as far as Narrawong where they pitched the tents. A boy had been bitten by a shark in a lagoon in only eight-inch deep water. It took eight stitches to seal the wound, they said.

Jonathan read to Alice from Hesse. *Siddhartha*'s river passages, the passage of river. The water flowed and flowed, constantly moving and yet always there, eternally the same and new at every moment! The passing of time, it no longer had any importance, what mattered was the summer, the fragrance of the sea, and basking in that feeling of eternal freedom of never-ending youth.

Ranco from Melbourne, born and raised in Yugoslavia, drove as far as Apollo Bay. His black sunglasses made him look like a dangerous insect.

They stopped at one of the most scenic spots on the South Coast, the Twelve Apostles. Deep below, a gigantic surf was pounding the rocks. For thousands of years it had been eating away at them, hollowing out, grinding down, eroding to sand. The ocean around Cape Otway is so ferocious that over time it has torn several ships apart.

"Steering a ship through these rocks," said Ranco, "was like trying to get a thread through the eye of a needle. The smallest mistake and your ship was gone. Take the Loch Ard, for example. It was one that got too close to the coast. The captain tried to anchor it so it wouldn't be tossed about any more, while he was setting sails at the same time, hoping that the ship would be blown out to sea. It hit a rock and sank within fifteen minutes. Only two people survived: Tom Pearce, a young sailor, and Eva Carmichael. She was Irish and traveling with her family to Australia. Tom only survived because he'd been able to hold on to a life boat. He was washed into a gorge, which still has the name of Loch Ard today. And Eva—she couldn't swim, but she was lucky to be able to hold on to a chicken coop, and when Tom saw her drifting out at sea, he jumped back in, swam toward her, fought the gigantic waves and finally managed to drag her to dry land. Both of them had spent almost five hours in the water. Tom then got help from a nearby farm and that's how they survived. End of story."

"And? What happened next? Did they fall in love?"

"No." Ranco took off his sunglasses and looked at Alice. "That only happens in bad novels and Hollywood movies. They never saw each other again. Eva sailed back to Ireland and Tom married another woman."

From Melbourne, they took the bus back to Sydney. Hitchhiking was too risky on that stretch, Ranco had told them. Several kids from abroad had been found butchered between Canberra and Sydney. Police were still looking for some of their limbs. "Do yourselves a favor," Ranco said, "and get a pair of bus tickets!"

First thing he did in Sydney was check for letters at the Poste Restante.

His father had written. If you're in trouble, he wrote, I will send money so you can come home. They were worried, he said, and wondering where he was, what had become of him. They wanted to know when he'd come home. Not a word about the pharmacy. But Dad needed to talk to him about Uncle Rudi.

They walked over to the Botanic Gardens. There it was again, Harbour Bridge, off to the side the Opera House, the cockatoos and the galahs. A sad mood assailed him. Somewhere deep down he sensed he was not to see all this again soon.

"See the arch?" Alice was pointing at the bridge.

"What about it?"

"It reminds me of an arc ball. You know, when you gently throw a basketball in an arc and it lands in the hoop with that sound of the perfect fit. Nothing more perfect than that. You know immediately when the ball leaves your palm, you know whether it'll miss the hoop. It's a gentle caress of the ball and the hoop."

"Sounds like a science."

"It's not. It's all about sensation and sensitivity. And you know what the opposite of the arc ball is?"

He sure didn't.

"The slam dunk." She seemed very serious all of a sudden.

"I have a wonderful uncle," said Jonathan. "In his youth he used to jump off the arches of bridges just like that one. Well, maybe not quite as high. Near our town there is a canal, it's called the *Mittellandkanal*, the midland canal that connects the Rhine with the Oder River on the German-Polish border. Uncle Rudi used to jump from its steel bridges."

The *Mittellandkanal* was like a muddy artery running through Germany disrespecting the death-bringing fences between West and East. Although Rudi had the vision of a hawk he was unable, as he got older, to see how deep the canal was. It wasn't so much the fault of his eyes as the fact that the canal had been a crystal-clear stream in his youth, while it was getting increasingly murky during the German economic miracle years. Owing to the canal's turbidity, when Rudi once again climbed to the top of the arch of the steel bridge and like a swallow threw himself over the sidewalk into the canal, he was forced to rely more on his memory of its varying depths than he could trust his eyes. He kept jumping even at an advanced age when his buddies were still teasing him about it. "Hey Rudi," they would say, "see that barge over there?" Of course, he could see the barge laden with black coal approaching the bridge from the West. "Can you still do it?" they teased him.

His drinking buddies would wink at each other, or even say:

"Hey old boy, at our age this might not be such a good idea anymore."

But Uncle Rudi could not be dissuaded from what he was about to do. He climbed to the highest point of the arch where he stood for a moment raising himself a few times on his toes. He jumped precisely at the moment when the front of the coal barge had disappeared behind him under the bridge. In a Jesus-on-the-cross-pose he flew out over the canal with his head aiming for the clouds rather than the water below. He slowly came round in a wide arch and broke the surface of the muddy water only a few feet in front of the barge, which then buried him underneath itself. There at the deepest point of the canal only inches under the keel of the barge he would lay low, his lungs half empty so that his body wouldn't rise, waiting until the barge had slowly passed over him. It was so dark down there in the deepest groove of the canal that he was unable to see the barge passing by, but he could feel its presence and he could hear it when it had cleared the water above him. Not until then did he surface, grinning proudly and relieved at the same time, for once again, at the age of forty-nine, he had escaped the deadly blades of the propellers. At least a dozen of his buddies applauded him from the bridge's sidewalk, over which he had jumped, and that was his reward, the recognition of his friends.

It was on one fine summer day when Uncle Rudi climbed the steel arch again, braced himself for his jump, launched himself toward the puffy clouds, and came down hard on the muddy waters of the canal. He noticed immediately that something wasn't right, and when he climbed out of the perfectly straight waterway to dry himself off he saw the bruises and swellings on his limbs and chest. Rudi had broken six bones in his body, two in his arms, two ribs, and two in his clavicle.

Would he settle permanently in Australia, Dad asked on the phone that night. How could he? His visa had reached its six-month halfway point. He had to leave. At least for a while. I'll come home soon, he said. Don't worry. Dad seemed relieved. Oh, but there was something else.

The doctors had finally figured out Rudi's strange condition. They called it the glass bone disease, for his bones would break as easily as thin glass. German doctors were always right and not known for creating false hopes in their patients. When Rudi asked them how much longer he had to live, they answered:

"Less than a month."

"Then I'd like to take my Audi out on the autobahn one more time."

It was Rudi's final wish, according to Dad.

"That's a bad idea," the doctors said. "In your condition, you could endanger not only your own life but also others around you."

One of Rudi's greatest passions was driving on the autobahn. Proudly he used to tell them when they were children that he had once again managed to drive his Audi Coupé in four hours from Munich to Hanover, a stretch that took the average mortal about eight hours. Whenever Rudi was seized by speed mania, he would start sweating profusely. It would start on his forehead until his whole face was dripping and his shirt and pants would turn dark with perspiration. He thought he owned the left lane. When a slower car temporarily left the right lane to pass another car, thus momentarily blocking Rudi's lane and endangering his record time, his sweat beads would spring as far as the dashboard, his hand would reach for his heart before resorting to flashing wildly at the trespasser, while his index finger was dancing madly on his moist forehead. It was the classical German gesture for referring to the stupidity of one's fellow citizens.

"Jerk," he yelled once the delinquent had left the lane and Jonathan wondered if the other driver was able to read his lips.

On the day he took his Audi out for the last time, in spite of the doctors' warnings, just after taking the exit from the autobahn, he threw out a banana skin, one of his last gestures to humanity, so to speak. He had already turned onto the country road and had just popped a fizzy vitamin tablet on his tongue when he noticed the light concert in his rear-view mirror and the banana skin sitting like a yellow star fish on the windshield of the highway patrol car.

"Have you been drinking?" the policeman asked him after he had rolled down the window.

"Yes," Rudi said meekly, some foam slipping from the corners of his mouth.

"How much?"

"Lots."

So they did a breathalyzer test.

When Rudi blew into the tube more foam was running out of his mouth and trickling down his chin. The test showed that he was completely sober, so the policeman asked:

"Didn't you say you've been drinking a lot?"

"Apple juice," Rudi said, the long word forcing a great deal of fizzy foam from his lips.

"Are you OK?"

"Yes, yes." Foam, foam.

"How come you're frothing at the mouth?"

"Jesus, it's from the fizz tablet I'm chewing. Just give me the damn ticket and let me go."

A flood of fizzy foam from the vitamin tablets was running from his face down and all over his Lacoste shirt, which amused the cop so much that he let Rudi go unscathed. At least that's what the policeman told Dad. After that, Rudi must have completely lost it. No doubt he took the Audi up to maximum speed on that country road, but whether he lost control or deliberately crashed into the solitary oak tree Dad did not know.

## Chapter 12
### *INNERLICHKEIT*

Inwardness

HER NAME WAS Hannah. She eyed him suspiciously. Supper was spent in silence.

He withdrew soon to his room. He wanted to be alone. He had loved his uncle dearly, had hoped to see him alive again, but now he was gone.

Their hushed voices still reached him.

"Is he good to you?"

"He's the sensitive kind," she was whispering. "We knew each other back in Germany. He came to Australia to look for me."

There was silence for a while.

"You know, I've got to see your uncle over there. Will you come with me? He specifically asked for you."

"But, Mom, you know I don't really want to go back there."

"I'm not so keen on going either, but it's no good avoiding things or people you don't want to face."

The next day he swung by the hostel he had stayed in when he first got to Australia. All his former roommates had left except Peter. The Kiwi was happy to see him again and asked him about his journey round the country. The time for his big trip had obviously not come yet. Maybe it never would. Maybe for some people dreaming about travel is a lot more pleasant than going through the hardship of actually doing it. In nineteenth-century Germany if you traveled you were considered *verrückt*, insane. It was an odd word, he thought, *verrückt,* literally meaning 'displaced.' Physical displacement perceived as leading to mental displacement.

He told Peter that he had to leave the country in a matter of days and was planning to go to New Zealand for a week or so before re-entering Australia for another six months.

Peter just snorted. "Don't do it," he said.

"What?"

"Don't go to New Zealand."

"Why not?"

"It's a lot more expensive than here even."

"So where should I go instead?"

"Asia, of course. Cheapest place on the planet and a lot more exciting than New Zealand. Head to China or India."

"I have a feeling you'll be back soon," Bob said on the eve of Jonathan's departure. He had made sure not to show up with Alice. She would have been some sort of giraffe to the cartoonist in him.

"I may not," he said to Bob. How could the uniqueness of a great adventure ever be reproduced?

As a parting gift, Bob gave him a small white and blue painting of his. It showed a muscular man bent so far over his head had disappeared up his own ass.

"I thought you might like this," Bob said with his typical grin.

"Are you trying to tell me something?"

"Yeah. Don't let your inward journey become too inward. It's a comment on the self-obsessed nature of some people. The Germans certainly qualify for it, wouldn't you say?"

Alice was excited about the idea of China. "Let's go. I've always wanted to see the Great Wall." They had a cappuccino next to a jukebox again. No dead moth in this one. The drop of a coin. The traveler gets a cross-section of life. The demands of life are the same wherever one goes. Love. Money. Youth's certainty in the importance of its own life. Hold on to it as long as you can. What a beautiful song. Herb Alpert. Your face by the candlelight. The luster of your eyes. The shyness of your smile. The surge of your hair. The music of your voice. *You say, this guy, this guy's in love with you. Who looks at you the way I do, when you smile?*

# CHAPTER 13
## *WELTGEWORFENHEIT*

Thrown out into the world. (German can do it in one word.)

WAS THERE SUCH a thing as a global songline?

The quintessence of leaving: there it was again, that old familiar feeling of being thrown out into the world: their *Weltgeworfenheit.* Like a boomerang at the farthest point before its return. And how could he translate *Geborgenheit* to her, that snug feeling of being sheltered in a place one called home. In those days, he thought, they found it in the altocumulus.

Just like him she was running from something, he couldn't tell what, and hadn't asked her about the conversation between Mother and daughter he had overheard, for he didn't want to reveal his eavesdropping.

On Air India: two Sikhs under the weight of huge turbans and Indian music mixed with Beethoven. The flight attendant, a woman with unconventional beauty, leaned over asking for meal orders: Chicken Breast Chasseur or Prawn Curry? Her words rolling like marbles off her tongue. The Indian world map in the in-flight magazine contained islands in the Mediterranean that did not exist. And far below passes the Vietnamese coast line, then a few paradise islands. Finally, the hair-raising landing in Hong Kong between fog-crowned mountains and skyscrapers.

They checked into the Chungking Mansions.

Slept on the rain tarps of their tents so the skin would not touch the mattresses. Once again, seven to one room—meant: nowhere to make love—among them a few bald European Buddhists. Alice whispered: "A journalist once asked Mahatma Gandhi: 'What do you think of Western civilization?' And you know what he said? 'It would be a good idea.'"

It took half an hour to Lo Wu, the border station. Loaded like mules, thousands are streaming across into the People's Republic. They're channeled into lines running toward a series of customs booths where the tyranny of the border awaits them, a foul-smelling sewage canal and a huge wall separating Hong Kong from China.

The special poetry of walls. With its several coils of barbed wire winding around each other like mythological beasts to deter the Capitalists from entering the Communist paradise, this wall reminds him of Germany's very own anti-Fascist protection wall that was soon to become a museum piece. The poetic tyranny also of forms: repeatedly, they're asked if they suffer from AIDS, or if they are psychotic. There are two currencies: the Foreign Exchange Certificates, FEC, for foreign psychotics, and the Renminbi yuan, the people's money, for sane natives. Banknotes showing a great sense of aesthetic appreciation: the orange fifty-yuan note, for example, shows the Li River flowing languidly through the cone-shaped limestone mountains of Guangxi Province, while on the smallest matchbox-sized renminbi bill surrounded by four languages a truck is working its way along a muddy road.

On the train to Guangzhou, Canton, their seat reservations turn out to be useless. As soon as they enter the compartment all seats are immediately snatched up by the happy crowd. How to survive on ten words of Chinese: *Hang Piao Leang*, he keeps saying standing in the middle of the train, leaning against Alice and pointing toward the landscape outside moving slowly past—rice paddies under a milky haze. Golden light flowing toward the horizon in the water puddles. *Hang Piao Leang*, it means *beautiful* and serves as the only currently available offering of friendship to a people they fail to understand. He repeats it several times—*hang piao leang*—on the train to Guangzhou to express his admiration for the landscape. The Chinese are smiling, the young girls are blushing. It's quite clear: these foreigners are all psychotic. Non-foreign eyes are glued to Alice towering in great solitude over everyone.

The other expression he knows is *Wo She Deguo Ren*: "I'm German."

As he barks these words into the crowd, it responds with looks of bewilderment among its youths and benevolent smiles from its elders. One Hong Kong Chinese keeps talking to them in English, looking around and making sure that everyone knows he's from the Western world. What is it that Jonathan does for a living, he wants to know, ignoring the possibility that Alice too might have a professional life. Jonathan tells him that traveling over the last six months he has learned more than in seven years at university. The young man replies: "There is a proverb in China that says that you learn more by walking ten thousand miles than by reading ten thousand books."

In Guangzhou/Canton they sleep on the island of Shamian Dao in the Pearl River. A dense humid haze hangs over the whole city. The setting sun no longer manages to penetrate the air thick with industrial fumes. Although Shamian Dao claims to be an island, it's connected with the rest of the city by several bridges. East or West? The communism of this area has little to do with the dark streets of Eastern Germany. The suburbs of Paris aren't much different. People here sit in streetside cafés drinking tea, their children playing on the sidewalks along the Pearl River.

Shamian Dao is a quiet place. It's almost cozy compared to the other parts of Guangzhou. The guidebook explains that its Western appearance is a result of the foreign influence it experienced throughout the eighteenth and nineteenth centuries, a time when British merchants settled in these parts and Guangzhou was China's only city able to trade with the rest of the world. The British traded opium and exported Chinese tea to England until, during the First Opium War from 1840 to 1842, China tried but failed to ban this trade, a conflict that was resolved through the Treaty of Nanjing and Britain's acquisition of Hong Kong. When other trading centers sprang up along the coast, Guangzhou finally lost its significance and its wealth. Only the great mansions of Shamian Dao and the broad avenues lined by large trees still evoke the time of prosperity.

You can buy two apples for the price of one night in a hostel here. Only the wealthy can afford to eat on Shamian Dao, so they cross over to the mainland and sit down at one of the street cookeries' small round tables. Here dry pink and bright yellow cakes are being sold, as well as soup from a huge vat, creamy gray soup, it looks like sewage but is deliciously sweet and only ten cents a bowl. The words for soup and sugar are almost identical, something like *tang*, the only difference being the pitch, the word melody. Alice gets it wrong each time and harvests bewildered looks from the vendors. There's amazing inflexibility when it comes to foreign accents. Getting the pitch only a tiny bit wrong means you're no longer being understood.

Here on the mainland the streets are clogged with people honking horns or ringing their bicycle bells, and everywhere beggars are lying in the dirt, their rags tied around leg stumps, or dragging themselves legless along the lanes, pushing in front of them hats displaying a few yuan notes. No stigma is attached to the act of begging here. Passers-by bowing down to give generously: something practically unseen in the polished pedestrian zones of Munich's inner city. The other beggars are the little snot-nosed kids clinging to Alice or jumping up and down with outstretched palms. Where are their parents? Three-year-old girls, their eyes reflecting a much riper age, are slipping motherless through this crowd. Alice gives one of them a coin, and instantly she is surrounded by a dozen more.

Horses' heads: a new smell. Missing their skin and hide, these heads pile up in baskets, attracting flies. Are they messengers from the underworld? An old man bends over the red and white heads digging his forefinger into one of the eye sockets. He scrapes out a bit of fat, inspects it with intensity. But nobody looks at him. Instead, as usual, they're all looking at Alice. Her private space is reduced to an absolute minimum. Surrounding her by the dozen, they stare in utter amazement at her huge pack and the seven-league boots, then at him, his black leather jacket, the torn jeans, and the sneakers.

His fourth pair by now.

Old women are approaching Alice, trying to reach up to her red-brown curls and drive their bony hands through her hair, snaking around her broad shoulders. Medusa. They're watching these *gweilos* watch the restaurant cages containing many of those animals that Western pet shops sell to people who love and feed them until the day they die from natural causes: rabbits, hedgehogs, turtles, rats, guinea pigs, pythons, pigeons, and swallows, even a badger. His cage is so small that if he wants to move he has to turn around himself. Gone bonkers from his long imprisonment, the badger keeps swiveling around his own center like a top, biting his posterior. Another psychotic. No doubt the best thing that can happen to him is to get eaten as soon as possible. For a moment, he stops and looks at them with intelligent eyes. The hair on his back is standing on end, then, in a flash, he jumps back into his vicious circle. A young man approaches them and asks Jonathan in broken English if he wants to eat snake. Sixty yuan for a small poisonous snake.

"How do you eat a small poisonous snake?"

"Very easy," he says, "you cut head off, spill fresh warm blood in glass of wine, then drink it. You believe me, it has magic effect on manpower."

He winks and nudges Jonathan's elbow conspiratorially.

"Then you fry meat and eat it. The more poisonous snake the better meat for manpower. You eat my snake, I guarantee you, your woman will love you fo'ever."

Jonathan passes on the snake blood.

"How much for the badger," asks Alice.

The man looks at her in surprise.

"You want to eat? It's family dish."

"Maybe."

"Five hundred yuan."

"Does that include the cage?"

"Six hundred with cage."

"Done."

They spend hours trying to find a large enough park where chances are good that the badger would not be caught again the next day. Finally—Alice opens the cage door but the badger keeps turning inside. Come on, she says tilting it slightly. He slips out snarling at his savior. From force of habit he keeps turning a few more times, then stops, looks around, in shock at the sudden availability of space, and disappears into a bush.

The boat along the Pearl River to Wuzhou passes from the heavily industrialized plains into the mountains. "Hard berth" means a small wooden bunk with a bamboo mattress. The only thing more Spartan would have been third class, bunks on deck separated from each other through thin plywood partitions. There is a lot of sitting and drinking, gobbling and smacking, belching and spitting down into the river, and licking plates clean. Without interruption, garbage is thrown into the river. The food keeps coming on trays full of steaming bowls of noodle soup.

The area around Guangzhou has a feeling of consummate sadness. The leaden skies weigh upon the brown river surrounded by industrial plants, smokestacks, cranes, and electricity poles. Ships are rusting away in the dirty water and crumbling factories of brown brick. The only idyllic detail is the presence of the long thin wooden boats gliding over the river like Venetian gondolas. Freight ships built entirely of wood carrying baskets and coal, sand and wood chugging east. One of them carries a gigantic poster of Mao, a patch of soul-lifting red in this montage of gray. In the distance the hills appear, some lonely smoke stack sentinels barring the view, and on the river banks the usual bicyclists and pedestrians in their blue-gray suits barely stand out against the gray of the sky.

Toward evening the river is getting cleaner, the air holds a fragrance of pine, and cooler winds speak of snow-capped mountains.

Alice snuggles in closer.

"I'm glad we left those smokestacks behind. Mom would have freaked out if she'd seen them. The badger in the cage would have spooked her too."

"Why?"

"I suppose it's because she was stuck in the mine during the war. But it's also about an animal waiting to be killed. Waiting for the butcher."

Her face changes, darkens for a moment.

"You OK?"

"Yeah, sure. Was just thinking of something."

"How did your Mom survive in an underground passage? Was your uncle in there with her?"

"No, he wasn't."

"Was he not persecuted, like your mother?"

"He was the one who took her to the mine when things were getting bad for them. They had been safe for a while thanks to his profession as a doctor and the status and respect he was held in by the town leaders. He thought they were protected from the deportations. But when he realized that things were getting worse, he and a close friend of the family took Mom to her shelter. My uncle was then deported only a few days later."

"Where?"

"To Auschwitz."

"And he survived that?"

"He never reached it."

Suddenly there's a lot of commotion on the boat. Alice takes his hand and they swim with the crowd.

The sky is clearing and the farthest summits are dipped into an orange sunset, somewhere over the glacial expanses of Tibet. The passengers are hypnotized by the sight of *shan*, the mountain world. The river is getting greener, winding between rounded peaks with trees growing all the way to the top.

The next morning they take the bus from Wuzhou to Yangshuo, a stretch of less than three-hundred kilometers. It takes twelve cold hours. Somewhere in a small town, in early morning light, a group of old men and women are doing their Tai Chi exercises in perfect synchrony. After a few hours, the bus stops at a roadside vegetable stall where fresh bamboo is sold.

"It's supposed to work like dental floss," Alice says, quoting the guidebook.

Looking at the toothless saleswoman, who is no older than thirty, it is tempting to question the validity of that statement. The woman wants three FEC for one of the green foot-long specimen. Alice is about to pay when the old woman next to the young one—her mother?—shows her spotless teeth and lets all hell break loose. She hands Alice back a stack of banknotes in return for the two FEC she has given her. Proud of her honesty she winks conspiratorially as if she were saying: "Look at me, I showed her, didn't I; no reason to cheat on someone just because he's clueless about our language and culture."

Bamboo is eaten panda-style. Imitating her fellow travelers Alice holds the stick in front of her like a sword and starts tearing off its fibers, sucking them dry.

The cold makes his bladder scream. Their packs are on the roof of the bus, so it's impossible to get a sweater. They lean against each other to get warmer but the pressure is on. Desperately, he is leafing through his phrase book in search of the Chinese word for "pee," "urination," or "toilet." He finds "toilet" in its Roman transcription and repeats it to himself several times before heading up to the driver, looking at him pleadingly while uttering the word and pointing to his crotch. The driver does not get it.

So he says the word over and over, enunciates it, starts yelling, it's all in vain, the driver just cannot penetrate this psychotic accent. He keeps grinning and nodding wildly but then looks back at the road and keeps going. For two more hours he has to suppress his urge to pee on the floor already redolent with bodily refuse, when suddenly the bus screeches to a halt and lets off a few passengers at a tiny village.

Jonathan runs to the door, jumps out, and rushes randomly into a small lane, positioning himself in a farm yard, unzips and relieves his pressure against a wall. Halfway through his urination, he is discovered by two villagers. They come running toward him, wildly waving their arms in the air and yelling madly *buchwe buchwe*, no, no. It's all rather intimidating. Zip and off through the lane, back to the road, without looking back a single time.

He freezes. Looks down the empty road, but the bus is gone.

What else was there to do but start walking in a northerly direction. Yangshuo was another sixty kilometers away. He was wishing now, of all times, he had his biography of Gerstäcker to hand. But it was safely packed away in his bag on the bus with Alice.

Her last words still echoing through his mind. He had asked about her uncle again and why it was that he never reached Auschwitz? It was thanks to Hermann, a close friend of the family. He was much older than her uncle and had served in the First World

War. A man who had friends in high places, although he wasn't really a Nazi, according to her uncle, just someone running with the pack. Hermann had offered to look after her mother when she was hidden in the mine, and her brother Wolfram had always claimed that it had been thanks to Hermann that the train was stopped on its way to Auschwitz, and that her uncle was taken off it and sent to Theresienstadt, where survival was more likely than in Auschwitz.

He heard an engine rumbling, tires crunching. The bus stopped right next to him.

"No need to walk," she yelled from the window. "Guess what: I was actually able to tell the driver that he'd lost you." She held up his Chinese-English phrasebook. So far he'd been the one in charge of communication.

Yangshuo, Guangxi Province.

In the market square, clusters of old men in blue-gray suits are having lively discussions, their hands folded on their backs. The pink fluorescent caps of the children and heaps of yellow grapefruit stand out garishly against the black village pond and the dark garment of the adults. The backdrop to a landscape of timeless beauty. Thousands of densely wooded and fog-shrouded limestone mountains tower above fertile fields, like dragon teeth, some of them connected, others standing alone like solitary cones under what seemed to be an ever-gray sky reflected by the languidly meandering Li River.

After a cold shower they walk around the village. Alice haggles down the price for a black second-hand coat to feel warmer, but also to be less noticed because of her Western clothes. A great variety of food is being sold on these small streets. The only fruit though seems to be that pear-like giant grapefruit sold in nets of four. A traditional delicacy of Guangxi Province is steamed rat, a dish the government recommends as part of a campaign trying to master the rat problem. Dead rats are being sold all over the market square, the merchants squatting in front of them grabbing them by the tails before placing them onto newspapers used as wrapping paper.

They took refuge in Lisa's Café.

He asked the young couple at the table next to them what it is that they're having.

"It's called 'Three Squeals,'" the guy says, his English accent heavily French.

"What is it?"

"It's live baby rats," he says, grinning sardonically. "They squeal three times before they get eaten. The first time they squeal when you pick them up with the chopsticks, the second time when you dip them into soy sauce, and the third time when you bite the heads off."

He and Alice order fried rice.

He hears them whisper: "*C'est les americains, sans doute. Absolument aucune culture. Mangent avec des fourchettes.*"

"What did they say?" Alice whispers.

"They think we're Americans. They're mocking us because we're using forks instead of chopsticks. They said it's typical of Americans, that we have absolutely no culture."

"Really? They actually said that?" she says a bit louder. The French are looking over. Turning to them she goes: "Do you want to know why I eat with a fork?" They look a bit intimidated. "I do this," she continues in disdain, "to protect the rainforests, so that I don't contribute to logging and the destruction of the environment just for those chopsticks you'll eat with once before they're tossed away."

In Guilin, they ask about trains from Guyang to Chongqing. It is impossible to get any information on ten words of Chinese, but from what he understands from the gestures and the word war is that they would first need to go to Guyang, fifteen hours away, to find out about trains going further north. The next train is not until eleven p.m., time to escape into a ritzy hotel to catch a break from the grime and the stares. And, of course, to rest before the train ride itself.

They keep traveling in hard-seat class. As soon as the gates open the race for the seats explodes—kicking, pushing, weaseling, and running, a fight of Darwinian proportions that makes you give up immediately.

"You sure we want to get on this train?" Alice yells at him above the buzzing of the crowd.

"We have to. Just wait until they're all inside," he yells back.

Another big mistake.

The hard-seat class fills within minutes, not just with people but also with all their belongings; there's no choice but to stay between the cars close to the doors, where, on a potato sack, some travelers have already found relief from standing. He wonders what sixteen hours of standing in the cold space between the compartments was going to do to their bodies and minds. His instinct tells him to sit down on their packs if it were not for the floor full of tangerine peels and peanut shells fermenting in yellow-green expectoration.

Thick tobacco smoke fills the whole train. There are no non-smokers among these men. They must think him an anomaly. Repeatedly they try to offer him a cigarette, his refusal triggering looks of incomprehension. Directly in front of him, there's a samovar with hot water. It's the chief cause of the constant commotion of the crowd as people keep filling up their tea glasses. Under the samovar twitches a rat tail. One that got away from the cooking pots. Or the Pied Piper. All plunged and perished, save one, stout as Julius Caesar swam across the river Weser. The animal jumps out of its hiding place only to disappear again behind two potato sacks. Boiling water is poured into the glasses, immediately creating light green tadpole ponds in which the tea leaves are dancing like newborn amphibians.

One of the ticket collectors is hitting a man, pulling him by the hair. The young man is close to tears, green snot running from his nose, and he is clinging to his thermos flask—the very bone of conten-tion—since he tried to fill it up at the samovar, thus claiming more water for himself than is appropriate. One of the cooks joins the con-ductor and both of them are now pummeling the delinquent. Aware of the embarrassment they're causing they signal to Alice, Jonathan, and four men from Hong Kong to move down the train into the restaurant car.

It's a moment of respite.

They breathe in the clean air of the empty car for half an hour. Then it's back to hard-seat class. He treads lightly in constant fear of slipping on the puddles of phlegm—of being forced to touch them with his hands like the legless boy he saw pushing himself through the crowds at Guangzhou. No relief ever from touching the street gunk. The eating never stops. And yet, his eyes are magnetized by their soup bowls filled with what looks inedible but seems to be very tasty, moving its consumers to raucous laughter, even singing. As his most faithful friend, claustrophobia, is nagging away at him, he fails to comprehend how most people manage to remain so cheerful in the face of this constant lack of space.

He can feel himself getting sick. They make a run for the restaurant car again. The conductor had forgotten to lock it. Nobody seems to mind; on the contrary, the cook even offers them a soup containing an aimlessly drifting assortment of meaty lumps. It is his most intimate hope that they're porky bits, for they surely don't taste like beef, chicken, or any other civilized slaughter animal, but, of course, he realizes the possibilities are endless and the little bones and gristle he is trying to chew fail to remind him of the heavy bone structure of a sow. He and Alice are savoring these soups as slowly as possible so as not to be sent back to the hard seats too soon, not to be forced to be standing again, because from all that standing his thigh bones have dug deeply into his poor pelvis, making him lose even more in body height. He is aware that he has turned into a veritable dwarf next to Alice.

The ruse of slowly eating their soups fails, and too soon they find themselves back in the cattle cars. A miraculous landscape is slowly pulling past them. The train moves so slowly, it would be possible to run alongside it and not miss it. The mountains around here are much higher than in Yangshuo, with jagged peaks towering above a subtropical vegetation: banana trees, bamboo forest, rice paddies and fields of yellow rapeseed. Again and again, the train stops without any apparent reason, for half an hour, one hour, two hours, before resuming its journey ever so slowly.

After another two hours among the hard seats, Alice suddenly drops her chopsticks. She is deadly pale, her eyes severely bloodshot. Plowing her way through to one of the conductors she manages to somehow make him understand with the help of the four men from Hong Kong that she cannot go on like this any longer, that she desperately needs a ticket for a spot in sleeper class.

She has abandoned him.

An old man has spotted his misery and hands him a cup of jasmine tea. Jonathan's eyes cling to the distant peaks as do the lonely canopied cypresses up there. It baffles the mind. This landscape looks precisely like the ones depicted on countless silk scrolls. Rather than resulting from poetic transfiguration, they did in fact imitate reality. After a further three hours of standing, he starts walking through the train again, pushing past sweaty bodies reluctant to move and faces staring hard at him. He works his way through several cars full of hard seats until he gets to the rather more privileged travelers in hard sleepers. Who said that China was a classless society? This class is divided into smaller compartments, with each one of them containing six five-foot long wooden bunks. The top ones just below the ceiling are the cheapest due to the steep climb and the absence of a view from the window. Six bunks though do not mean six people. Each bunk serves a whole family to sit on so that the phrase "hard sleeper" is a complete misnomer. He keeps walking, past Alice, to the end of hard sleeper class. As he is trying to worm his way into soft sleepers, a hard-to-judge railway functionary breaks his stride and barks him back in the direction whence he had arrived.

In Alice's compartment he finds a tiny spot right next to her on her hard bunk bed. Three young men sit across from her.

*Wo she Deguo Ren*, he says to them, completely exhausted: I'm German.

Failing to understand they're eyeing him suspiciously.

*Wo she Deguo Ren*, he repeats very slowly raising his voice a little.

For a moment, the three young men remain perfectly immobile. Then they pick up a lively conversation, whipping each other with words until one of them has turned completely purple and starts yelling and gesticulating at the others, while staring at Alice and him from manic eyes. Smiles of ancient wisdom fly only to the old. The young man seems extremely agitated. His eyes wide open, all of a sudden his arm flies up, his hand shoots out, stretches out, then again, and again.

It was the perfect *Heil Hitler* salute.

Jonathan is in shock. A feeling of fear grips him. What if they think he is a neo-Nazi? Did Germans die first in China too?

The three of them look at him as if he were carrying Germany's complete guilt upon his weary shoulders.

Alice gives him a kiss.

"See? You can never get away from it," she says smiling. "Your past will follow you wherever you go. It does to my mother, too. When she first arrived in Australia, she thought she was in paradise. And that she'd forget her home, which never really was a home. Turns out she never did."

"And your uncle? How did he survive?"

"He stayed alive in Theresienstadt because he was a skilled doctor. He was sent there deliberately so he could treat some of the Nazis who had tuberculosis. That's why they took him off the train to Auschwitz. He was a known specialist for that disease. As soon as he arrived in Theresienstadt he was put in charge of the tuberculosis ward. Strange irony of fate, isn't it? The victim who treats the perpetrators. Who is forced to care for them. In the purely medical sense, of course. I think his friend Hermann may have had something to do with his rescue from the gas chambers."

"Theresienstadt. It wasn't a death camp, right?"

"Not like Auschwitz, no. Officially it was known as a Jewish settlement. But it was a transit camp really, for people to be deported on to Auschwitz and other extermination camps. My mother told me once that they had even disguised the camp as a beautiful spa town, when representatives of the Red Cross were visiting to check on conditions there. There was a documentary made about this, which the Jewish prisoners ironically called *Der Führer schenkt den Juden eine Stadt.*"

"And Hermann? What happened to him?"

"He's dead now. It's odd, but Mom does not like to talk about him."

He kisses her cheek, feeling the eyes of their travel companions upon them.

"You know that my father asked me to come back to Germany? He's worried about me. I'm actually very worried about *him.* I need to check on him."

"What's wrong with him?"

"He's got heart problems."

"So does my mother. She actually just flew over there, to be with my uncle."

"What do you think? Should we head to Germany after Beijing? I could check on Dad and you could see your mother and uncle."

"I don't know," she says frowning. "I've always avoided going back there. Mom said the other day that she wants me there, but . . ."

"But?"

"I don't know."

"You've never told me why you left so suddenly back then."

She seems lost in thought.

"I'll tell you some time."

"You know, I did think about you a lot all these years."

"How come you never wrote or called?"

"I suppose my mother's hatred of Germany did not help when I grew up. Mentioning the place was almost a taboo."

"But why then did they send you on that school exchange?"

"That was my uncle's idea. He used to tell Mom that you have to let the past be the past and move on in life."

Chongqing is a blur. He's certain he is close to death. Vaguely he remembers her carrying him up the steps of the hostel, packing him into bed, her face hovering above his. For several days, his fever will not come down. She is nursing him with Chinese vodka. He's not sure what the cheap vodka is killing, the source of his illness or just him.

While he's confined to his sick bed, Alice has befriended Andi, a British fish specialist. As a foreign expert, he has lived in Chongqing for nearly a year. Nobody knows fish the way Andi does. One night, when he's started to feel much better, they accompany Andi to some of his friends for a local delicacy: fresh eel from the Yellow River. Inside a hole in the middle of their large table, there's a sort of fondue pot, in which a chili sauce is simmering. The beers arrive, then the river eels, all of them alive, of course, how could they be fresh otherwise? Dead is always second-degree fresh. Thank God, he thinks, these eels are small; if they were the size of his arm like the one in Günter Grass's *The Tin Drum* he'd go back to bed for another week.

Hundreds of them are assembled in a large wok, wriggling round each other like Alice's hair in the wind, worming, snaking, and eeling around with sleek, twitching bodies, as if they knew what was coming.

"They're delicious fish," Andi promises, "you have to try them. Our hosts will be insulted if you don't. It's very easy. Just put a few bean sprouts and cucumber pieces into the sauce, then you sink your chopsticks into the eels, you pull one out, dip it into the boiling sauce, just briefly, so it's not quite dead yet when you pull it out again. It still needs to wriggle a bit when you eat it, so it stays fresh in your mouth and won't die until you chew it. Remember: just a few seconds in the sauce."

Like furious Aesculapian snakes, the eels are writhing round the chopsticks, soon, however, losing their love of life in the simmering sauce, twitching one last tired time before the mouth welcomes them, their little bones breaking with a crunch, a fleeting impression of fish, and down the throat they slide.

Their hosts are happy with them. One of them, a young man with a very red face, speaks a few words of English. Raising his glass to Alice, he obviously mistakes her for an American, maybe because of her size:

"Bush Good Man." He downs the tsingtao, fills his glass again, and raises it to Jonathan: "Rummenigge Good Man."

Then he starts pummeling Andi with a volley of words. Andi has to translate:

"He says he's a student and has been persecuted by the government since the days of Tiananmen Square. He suggests that you," turning to Alice, "send him a letter from the United States inviting him officially to visit you there."

The young man offers him a cigarette, *buchwe buchwe*, but he keeps trying at least five times.

"They don't take *no* for an answer," Andi says. "Saying *no* is just a polite way of saying *yes*."

Suddenly, the ninety-year-old hostess starts fingering his jeans. Instinctively, he moves closer to Alice. The old woman is mumbling a word.

"Did she say fuck?" he asks Andi whose mouth is full of dying eel.

"She said luck. She said you're in luck. She wants to darn those holes in your pants, but only on the condition that your wife will send her grandson that letter."

They leave the next day on a boat from Chongqing heading down the Yellow River, through the three famous gorgeous gorges, all the way to Yichang. From there the choices are either standing for twenty-eight hours to Beijing or spending three hundred and thirty FEC for the Soft Sleeper. Alice gives up immediately and buys herself a ticket for the soft sleeper.

"I've had enough of those cattle cars," she says. He can't afford anything else, though. She gives him a kiss and stays for a while. She could have gone ahead and stayed in a clean and quiet waiting room, her ticket includes this luxury as well as a reservation for her bed, but she decides to stay with him. His nerves are frail after all this traveling. She must have noticed it.

At least fifty men and women are crowding them again. It's impossible to have a conversation. The women are touching Alice's hair and the men pointing at his torn jeans or fingering his leather jacket. All of a sudden he just explodes. Starts screaming: "Why do you keep staring at us? And what's so funny about us? Are we in a zoo here, or what? Why don't you start minding your own business instead of bothering us!"

She puts her hand on his lower arm to calm him. Their fellow travelers are all highly amused by his emotional collapse, his Western hysteria, but he feels a lot better. It was necessary, so he could regain his composure, he had merely opened a valve and was almost in a good mood after this Teutonic outbreak. No one is staring at them now, the gates have opened and everyone is running to the train again.

Alice and he are temporarily separated. Although he is about to be standing for the next twenty-eight hours he feels completely reconciled with the Chinese. They notice his friendly inclination and return it with the usual curiosity. With the help of his phrase book, he is trying to explain to them that he was in Australia but is really from Germany.

*Wo she deguo ren, wo she deguo ren.*

They pass around the phrase book inspecting it with keen interest, and he keeps attempting to tell them that China is a very beautiful country—*hang piao leang*, very nice, *hang piao leang*, hell, why are the young girls blushing again. A young man with good English smiles and says: "not *hang piao leang*, means beautiful in context of young woman, say *mai-lee* instead."

He stays standing through the night, his hips screaming. Finally, dawn creeps over the land. He recognizes a few mud villages, steam engines on distant tracks, their smoke eating away at the steel gray sky, a donkey dragging a rickety cart next to the train. The land is completely flat. His shoes are too and covered in slime to boot. Almost impossible to get through this crowd. He steps on their feet, they move a little, they sigh a little. Clogged like the veins of a chain smoker. Impossible to breathe. No seats anywhere. Tired faces everywhere. They're used to it.

At least Alice looks rested.

Morning sunshine in this dull, flat land. So far nobody has noticed his intrusion into soft sleeper class, but they're approaching Beijing, and toward the end of any train journey the boundaries between the classes become porous. There's a clean toilet here and running water, the beds are covered with spotless white linen and the pillows are handcrafted. He manages to rest for an hour before the train attendant sends him back.

Standing for a few more hours, he tries to relax by looking out the window onto the distant horizons of this mirthless landscape. More and more, the land has filled up with heavy industry, with electricity poles as far as the eye can see, then, with the suburbs of Beijing, gray huts under a leaden sky.

Central station. The crowds are pushing toward the exit. Fresh air, finally, and cold too, cutting into skin. The smell of snow. The cab drivers throw themselves upon the newly arrived. One of them puts up four fingers. What's four fingers? Four kilometers, four FEC to the Hotel District? He nods, yes, four FEC to hotel, wherever the hotel is. They drag their packs to the bus, then he adds, slurping his tea, that it's forty. Forty FEC. No energy to argue. Alice pays the Western price.

He makes a long overdue phone call home. Mom says he should come back soon. Dad's health. The heart. The valve. She sounds depressed. Where? China? What on earth? Was he out of his mind?

They head to the Great Wall through thick snowflakes. Climbing its steep passages, the famous steps have transformed into icy slides.

Suddenly Alice's scream behind him.

She's slipped.

"Dammit," she screams in pain. "That fucking knee."

With amazing agility, she jerks it back into place.

She leans on him all the way back to Mutianju, where they go to see a doctor—an ancient man with a long pointed white beard. He bandages her knee and hands her a pair of wooden crutches. The biggest ones he could find, but she is still bent over. Like an Amazon returning from battle.

The doctor looks concerned. "You should rest for two weeks. Not walk much."

They could have stayed at the hostel. But he presses on. I have to go home, he says to her. I think Dad's in a bad way.

"We should take the train."

She was right. What better way to rest and see the world at the same time than taking the Trans-Siberian. The idea made her smile.

"But not standing," she says. "Sitting or lying down only."

The next morning, they line up outside the Russian embassy.

Two and a half hours. No success.

As they get to the gates, the embassy closes. Whoever doesn't get in between nine and one has to come back the next day and line up even earlier. A few Germans try to jump the queue. One of them is a skinny guy with round glasses and a mop of curly hair. He seems to be in a great hurry, understandably, for if you missed the Trans-Siberian you had to wait for another week. The Germans may think that China is a land where jumping the line is no problem but they haven't considered the Russian guards positioned outside the embassy. In Russia, nobody jumps the line. The guards unshoulder their guns. Intimidated, the skinny guy steps behind his girlfriend.

They're back the next day. So are the German and his girlfriend. After three hours, during which nobody has moved an inch, the German loses it. The two menacing Siberian guards have been *davai-davai*-ing the German several times to get back in line. All of a sudden, he bursts out crying and coughing. Between sobs, he tells the guards in German that he is sick of waiting, that he's in desperate need of a visa to get back to Berlin, and above all that he doesn't see the point in talking to them in any language other than German, since they don't seem to be inclined to talk to him in any language other than Russian. The brawny Siberians are wetting themselves with laughter at the sight of the weeping German, whose girlfriend is trying to comfort him, but without success. He is stammering something about destiny having conspired against him.

She whispers: "We've been traveling in China for six weeks. About three weeks ago, his nerves snapped. He's been in bad shape ever since."

Her vacant stare. Then, almost solemnly, she says: "We followed a dream I had six months ago. A voice told me I should go to Huangshan, the holiest mountain of China, the mountain of the poets."

"And? Was it worth it?"

"Who knows? Time will tell. But it was freezing up there and Martin caught a bad cold."

"I'm sure he'll get over it. So now it's back to Germany?"

"Yes," she said. "Though going back there always feels to me like dying a little."

# CHAPTER 14
## *TAUWETTER*

The Great Thaw

THE MOMENT THEY sat down a square but somehow ageless woman entered the compartment with a determination that reminded him of the engine at the front of the train.

"*Ya provodnik,*" she growled.

He looked at her helplessly.

"*Ya provodnik,*" she yelled, seemingly convinced that any foreigner would understand Russian if it was yelled. She was the train attendant escorting them into Siberia. Shooting out deep gutturals, she was trying to administer a set of bed sheets. They were obviously in her way. Alice's size and her crutches seemed to bother her immensely.

The compartment consisted of four red upholstered bunk beds that could be tilted back against the wall. There was a small table by the window, red floor carpets, and a samovar. After the Chinese trains with their hard-seat class, this setting seemed to be pure luxury, although the heat was unbearable. He tried the windows but they were tightly shut and could not be moved from their locks. There would be no escape from this train.

Stripped to the waist, they tried to get some sleep on top of the sheets. A few hours later, they woke at Shenyang Station, greeted by yet another cold blue day in March. Thick smoke loitered on frozen platforms. To wash his face and arms, he filled his trail-worn plastic water container halfway with hot water from the samovar and added cold water from the tiny spigot in the toilet room. He then poured everything over his head and into his armpits. Neither he nor Alice had thought of bringing soap.

Outside, the land was flat and yellowish. There were small solidly frozen puddles and black smoke from ominous stacks coiled into the big bright blue. The brown towns they passed through looked as if they had been hit by bombs, their people huddling between big heaps of black coal.

At Changchun, he jumped out of the train to wipe the window, the *provodnik* snapping at his heels, yelling and motioning all the while that he should get back on the train.

His mission was fruitless anyway. The windows could not be wiped, neither from the inside nor the outside as the humidity sat right between the two glass panes.

The smell of coal intensified at Harbin, its people dressed in multiple layers, wearing anything they could lay their hands on. A fresh cover of snow clung to the black carriages and steam engines on nearby tracks. The map showed a land of great swamps. The next time he looked up, a flat brown short-grass steppe stretched as far as the eye could see. Tufts of light brown grass were strangled by the ice. A few skeleton trees scratched the sky. Behind them the setting sun ball, as red as a traffic light.

They arrived in Manzhouli. Mongolia was less than a mile to the left. Customs people got on the train and handed out Russian entry forms. Crossing the border into the Soviet Union was a five-hour process. They got off on the other side, only two fences away from China, and stood around with the Russians. These people's words and gestures flowed with great beauty and when they spoke their eyes were half closed. They seemed to let their language linger on the tip of the tongue caressing and rolling it around in saliva before releasing it to the sharp Siberian air. Their faces were rigid. While the Chinese were quick to laugh and grimace, these Russian faces were like the frozen landscape all around them. As if to laugh was to be on Satan's side.

There was no getting off of this train for another five days, all the way to Moscow. In the *vagon restoran* he glanced at a newspaper in the seat next to him. It was dated January 20, 1991, two months earlier. The menu on the table offered a variety of meals, bread and cheese, soup with sausage and sour cream, and beef stroganoff. He pointed at this, that, and the other but the waiter, a sweaty man in an unkempt uniform, made a face that was apologetic and mischievous at the same time.

"Today. Beef Stroganoff. Two Rubli."

Today thirty rubles was roughly one dollar. The exchange rate changed wildly from day to day. A full meal under ten cents: he'd never eaten so cheaply. Granted, the dish of Beef Stroganoff consisted only of three small pieces of gristle, a scoop of mash, and next to no sauce, but they were happy when the little aluminum dishes were placed in front of them. The waiter even brought two glasses of a grim-looking liquid.

"Juice," he said.

"Very bad," said the guy at the next table shaking his head and pointing at the glass.

As Alice was about to raise it to her lips, the waiter suddenly reappeared, grabbed it from her, and put down two new glasses.

"Apple juice," he said.

The guy at the next table just shook his head.

The heat was a killer. The only windows that could be opened were the ones belonging to the doors of the restaurant car, where passengers cooled down their flushed faces. Snow caps covered the distant yellow hills and telegraph poles ran along the tracks to the north. No other sign of human life out there.

"You have sweaters, *jeansey* or T-shirts you want to sell?" The waiter's name was Slavo, and he was eager to do business. Jonathan told him they had been traveling for a year, that their clothes had seen better days, and that probably he, Slavo, would not be interested in torn jeans or worn-out shirts.

"Well," Slavo said, "at least we can drink."

And to Alice: "You, what country? America?"

"Australia."

"Ah," he sighed with an exaggerated accent lengthening each vowel and rolling up his eyes with great theatricality: "Everlasting sunshine."

He looked her up and down for a moment. "What state?"

"New South Wales."

"Ah," he raised his eyebrows knowingly: "Melbourne."

He trudged along to the compartment where two new travelers had arrived, Alexej and Vadim, Don Cossacks from the town of Rostov na Donu. They were on their way home from the Chinese border. After sizing each other up suspiciously, Alexej uncorked a large goatskin sack and poured some clear liquid into five tea glasses. He filled them to the rim and cut off big chunks from a salami the size of a baseball bat. Jonathan tried to tell him that they had just eaten but they insisted that he and Alice eat some more before drinking.

"Homemade vodka. Never drink it and not eat salami," Slavo said. He was right.

The drink blazed a trail of fire down his throat while the three men watched him intently to see whether his face would twitch.

"Homemade vodka," Slavo said again, this time in perfect German. His eyes were as blue as the winter sky.

"You speak good German."

"Ah. *Nyet*. Funny German. My grandmother Volga German."

Jonathan pointed to the window. "Beautiful land out there."

"Ah. *Nyet*. Shit country."

The glasses kept filling and everyone's head was turning purple. The red carpet was getting soaked with sweat. After about an hour of talking to the two Don Cossacks, Slavo turned around, put his hand on Jonathan's leg and said: "I must go work. Not much. Just little."

He got up to go. Alice started digging around in her backpack. Slavo sat down again. Like hawks they followed every single one of her moves. She produced the bottle of vodka she had bought in Chongqing on the Yangtze River, poured some out, and offered it to the Russians. Putting it to their noses Slavo and Alexej looked at each other. They shook their heads and poured the liquid back into the bottle.

"Smell like shit," said Slavo.

"Dear Yanushka," he touched his leg again. His face was bathed in sweat, "I must work now. In Russia no tomorrow, live only today. I work a few hours, then come back. We have more vodka."

Alexej, the older Don Cossack, spoke a little English. He loved to talk about prices. How much for a pair of Adidas in Germany? How much for *jeansey*? How much for radio and how much for our tickets?

"Three hundred and fifty US dollars. All the way from Beijing to Berlin."

"Too much," he said. He had paid only sixty rubles, two dollars, to get from the Chinese border to Moscow. But it was all relative. Riding the Trans-Siberian was a three-tier system. For travelers coming from the West you had the official tourist prices that were in the thousands. Then there were unofficial prices for Westerners, especially those taking the train back to Europe from China. And then there were the Russian prices: two dollars for a ten-thousand kilometer journey. Sixty rubles was half a month's salary. Alexej and Vadim worked in a mine and each of them made one hundred and twenty rubles a month.

The vodka kept coming. Alice had long given up drinking it, and the two Cossacks seemed to accept this behavior in a woman. He, on the other hand, stood no chance and his glass kept refilling despite his protestations. It was getting dark outside. He could not fend off the thought that if he continued drinking this stuff he would not live to see Moscow. In the dim light of the compartment, he started pouring the vodka into a towel he had stuffed into the seat next to him. They did not notice.

It was Beef Stroganoff again. Slavo sat down with them and said how much he loved Germany. The land of poets, he said. He quoted Eichendorff and Heine, then some of Goethe's early poems, from an age when bourgeois thoughts were still far from his mind.

Slavo was a trained philologist. He had a PhD in literature, but in Russia there was no work at university, so he worked on the train. Besides, teachers were the worst paid people in the Soviet Union, so he preferred to travel on the great Siberian and meet foreigners with whom he could do business.

"Yanushka, slooshee," he said, "listen, if you have any Jeansee or T-shirts or Valuta, I get you Russian caviar or Champanskee. I can get you everything, *matryoshka*, you know Russian doll, you open one, another appears, only smaller, and so on and so on. I can get you Russian jewel box, no fake, guarantee, hand painted by monks. Or *shapka*, Russian hat. Made of bear. Rabbit. Rat. What you prefer."

Everyone wore these fur hats in the small Siberian villages

alongside the tracks. Villages full of snow, with unpaved roads full of gigantic frozen mud holes. But people lived in cozy-looking wooden cabins, from which the smoke puffed into the biting air. These dachas came in many colors, some of them with elaborately carved gables.

It was the end of March, yet no sign of spring anywhere.

The word got around quickly that there were some Westerners on the train. People were continuously passing by the compartment, looking in shyly. In the compartment next door sat a huge babushka. She wore felt slippers and reclined in a mound of pillows by the samovar gazing calmly at the land, a bunch of kids playing at her feet. Worn-out looking men in Adidas suits crowded the corridor. They were smoking heavily, their eyes on the endless landscape.

"*Biriosa*," said Vadim, who had watched Jonathan's gaze wander past the people in the corridor to the landscape outside.

*Biriosa*, that magic word for the Russian birch tree. The sun lingered on their trunks and their blue shadows languished on the snow.

Vadim had a hangover and dark shadows under his eyes. His hair stood in all directions, and he kept sucking his snot back toward his brain.

The landscape changed again when they got to the banks of Lake Baikal, the deepest lake on earth. To the south there were high mountains, beyond them still Mongolia. So far, they had both slept badly every night because of the shaking and jolting of the train. Every morning he and Alice woke up with massive headaches, from lack of sleep and too much vodka, and their stiff necks kept bothering them all day long. The mountains to the south came closer and closer, the number of birch trees increased, there were huge frozen rivers with jagged ice slabs sticking out in all directions.

On the third day, Alexej insisted they eat some of their homemade apricot jam. Once past Irkutsk, the train seemed to have run out of food.

"What about Beef Stroganoff?" Alice asked Slavo.

"It depends."

"On what?"

"How much you want to pay."

"In *roubli*?"

"*Nyet. Dollari.*"

His funds were running low these days and who knew what kind of food situation awaited them in Moscow.

"What about these prices here?" Alice asked pointing at the menu. "Beef Stroganoff for two *roubli*."

"*Nyet.* These prices for Russians only. You from the West."

"What about Solyanka?" she asked.

"*Nyet.*"

What about this, that, and the other? She kept pointing at the Cyrillic words on the menu that still had prices behind them, which meant they should have been available, but Slavo just shook his head. She asked him why all of a sudden there was no food anymore, but he just shrugged his shoulders and said:

"Bad time in Russia. People tired. Party don't care. Poverty everywhere."

"What about Gorbachev?" Alice asked.

He gave a quick snort of derision: "Before Gorbachev, we had chocolate. Now we have only Gorbachev."

The next morning revealed the secret of the food shortage on the train. They'd both wondered about the long lines of women on the platform every time the train made a stop. They carried bags with them but did not appear to be waiting to get on. Nor were they visiting relatives traveling on the train. There were just too many of them. Wrapped in their winter coats and their shapkas they were waiting patiently. But for what?

He found out on his way to the toilet, as he peeked through the small window of the locked door between their car and the *vagon restoran*. Slavo was busy handing small packages through one of the doors that opened out to the platform. So this was where all the food was going and why Slavo did not sell it to them. The women on the platform obviously paid better prices than the people on the train. While the prices on the train menu were official, Slavo's prices were probably much steeper, but the women were under pressure. It was still winter, the great thaw hadn't set in yet, and they would have had to wait another week if they had missed this opportunity. The Soviet Union was obviously drained of most food supplies. People were forced to hoard and grab every opportunity by the neck. He was starting to understand why the train coming through once a week was such a big event. It was a rolling market for the locals to restock on a bit of beef, cucumbers, and a few extra eggs.

They did not pursue the Beef Stroganoff discussion after this. Why invest their last dollars in some gristle with gravy? Alexej and Vadim were still feeding them their salami and apricot jam and their vodka, and there was also the glass of Nutella they'd bought from the Friendship Store in Beijing. Each of the four of them received a spoonful of the creamy chocolate butter every day. The train was now nearly drained of all supplies except for tea and maybe an egg, for a steep price. There was also that dim apple juice that tasted of anything but apples. Somewhere though, Jonathan could swear he smelled potatoes and gravy cooking, but Slavo, who'd given up on their last dollars, told him it was a fata morgana, a mirage.

"You're a German idealist," he said.

When Jonathan tried again, the smell of food was gone. Only coal and soot came in on the cold air rushing in through the open doors when the train stopped.

They kept going to the *vagon restoran* just to look at the menu and imagine what all they could eat if everything the menu showed were indeed available. Slavo came to sit down at their table:

"Ah. I very drunk yesterday." He pointed his finger to the ceiling: "Cosmos."

All of a sudden, on the fifth day there was some meat again. Tongue with an ounce of mash. Tongue had never tasted so good.

Back in the compartment, Alexej and Vadim opened a bottle of cognac and some wine. Everything they drank was poured down at one go, nothing was ever sipped unless it was sizzling hot. To sip alcohol seemed to be the ultimate in unmanliness.

The big babushka from next door walked past their compartment. She held on to the handrail that ran the length of the windows facing north. She looked out at Siberia, then started on her return journey to the compartment, where utterly exhausted she fell back into her pillows, the kids still playing at her feet. She was the Great Mother, her lap a huge cornucopia from which sprang forth Russia's new hungry children.

The menu said: Eggs and mayonnaise and the price hadn't been crossed out, which meant it should still be available.

"*Nyet!*"

"How about just eggs?"

"*Nyet!*"

"Then why's the price not crossed out?"

"Because we have mayonnaise. You can have that."

"For the same price as eggs and mayonnaise?"

"Of course. You from Australia and Germany. Does it hurt you?"

At all times, the *vagon restoran* was packed with travelers who would drink tea and keep hoping that an egg would one of these days be added to the mayonnaise, of which there was still plenty. In Tulun, two new waiters arrived. There was no telling why the train needed two waiters in addition to Slavo if there was no food to be served, but then again this was the Soviet Union where everybody had to be employed.

One of the new waiters walked up and down the corridor without ever changing the expression on his face. He was a complete stoic, ready to endure whatever fate would set in front of him. The other waiter had extremely greasy hair too long for his own good. As he walked through the overheated train a strand insisted on falling over his eyes, so that he had developed a sudden jerk of his head to throw it back into place. Unlike his colleague, this one was the classical Russian sufferer. His face had settled into a profoundly furrowed permanent scowl. He was like Oblomov, the Goncharov character, who'd fallen into deep despondence because he knew he could not change his fate. He and Slavo would sit down every once in a while, and drink vodka out of tea glasses, their faces purple and bathed in sweat. What a land of lonely souls touching in solitude, looked after by Father State and *Dyed Maroz*, that immortal Grandfather Frost returning relentlessly year after year to add to everyone's hardship.

One of the doors was open with the black landscape swooshing by. In the frosty air sat a kitchen boy, peeling potatoes.

The haggling and bartering never took place in the corridor. Instead, the compartment door was closed when Chinese T-shirts and sweat suits were touched, closely examined, and prices were set. Alexej and Vadim came back to the compartment, their faces beaming. They had just bought two pairs of Adidas sneakers for one hundred and twenty rubles each. One monthly salary, but they were worth it. Their shopping fever had not yet released them from its clasp, and they asked him how much he wanted for his boots. So he said: it's the only pair I have and if I sold it I'd be walking around Moscow barefoot, just like Ivan Bezdomny in *Master and Margarita*. That seemed to make sense to them, barefoot in Moscow in March, *nyet*, not a good idea, no matter how much moonshine vodka might be heating up his toes. So, they left his boots alone. As for his *jeansey*, they were so torn that even the Russians were not interested in them. In the West, where torn jeans were now the latest fashion, he could probably have sold them for more than the price of a brand new pair.

It was impossible not to go stir-crazy after being stuck on this train for close to a hundred hours. They had to get off by the time they reached Novosibirsk. The train stopped for fifteen minutes, *pyat natst minoot*. While Alice stayed on the platform to breathe the cold air, he walked out to the town square in front of the station, where a freezing Lenin statue and policemen in bearskin hats stared at him as if they had seen a ghost. There was a kiosk here that sold some cucumbers and eggs, but here too a long line of women had formed, coiling almost all the way around the square.

"*Nyet, nyet,*" snapped the *provodnik* when he returned, pointing at his wet boots, which left small puddles in her train. She had a gray metal bucket in her knotted hand and permafrost on her face. She threw a rag at him and motioned that he should wipe his feet on it. When he tried to use it to wipe the window she gestured that he should use his white Western T-shirt.

When she left, Alexej nudged him and winked.

"We go to *vagon restoran*. You and Alice want to be alone."

It's OK, he said, but Alexej insisted and winked again.

"I give you half hour."

It was the first time in a week that they were alone. They locked the door and drew the curtain.

Pink snow and the black silhouette of birch and pine under a purple band on the western sky appeared as they approached the Ural Mountains in the late afternoon of the next day. Thick birch tree forest hemmed both sides of the track. Then, finally, they passed the milestone that separates Asia from Yevropa. His heart made a little jump. The boomerang was homebound.

He changed some of his last dollars into Rubles. In their compartment everyone got jumpy. Slavo and his fellow waiters joined in. They closed the door and opened a new bottle of vodka. Alexej's and Vadim's goatskin bag with the moonshine was empty and so was the Chinese vodka from Chongqing. After the third day nobody had rejected it anymore. Their eyes shone with the booze and the prospect of being able to buy a VCR, a pair of jeans, or a leather jacket.

When the waiters were gone, Alexej, Vadim, Alice, and he shared their last spoonfuls of Nutella. Now that the glass was empty he wanted to throw it out but Vadim grabbed his wrist and held up a finger. He took the glass, filled it with hot water from the samovar and put it gently down on the table by the window.

They woke up in Yaroslavl, just a couple of hours from Moscow. Alexej and Vadim had disappeared.

"Did they get off the train?"

The train was pulling into the suburbs of Moscow when two guys entered the compartment. They did not recognize them at first. Alexej and Vadim had undergone a complete metamorphosis. They were groomed to within an inch of their lives, the smell of sweat had been replaced by heavy cologne, and they were dressed in their best Adidas suits and brand-new sneakers. Alice tried to express her admiration facially by nodding to them and raising her eyebrows. Alexej gave her a faint smile somewhat on the side of Satan and said:

"For our wives. We see them for the first time in two weeks."

Overnight, the few streaks of chocolate that had stuck to the inside of the Nutella glass had completely dissolved in the water,

which had adopted a slightly murky hue. Raising his glass to everyone, Vadim drank from it eagerly before passing it around.

# CHAPTER 15
*Heimlich* – secretly
*Heimisch* – homelike
(Not just Freudian concepts.)

AT BYELARUSKI STATION, Alexej said, you can go to sleep in the stationary cars.

"*Gdje spalny vagon?*" Jonathan asked a general, who looked at him as if he wanted to send him to the gulag.

Finding a place to stay in Moscow would have been impossible if they hadn't met Lucy. She sold candy and asked them in German whether they'd come directly from Germany.

"From China," Alice said. "On the Trans-Siberian."

She touched Alice's cheek and gave her a dozen lemon drops: "Here, my dear, eat these. You must be very hungry. In Russia for such a long time. Russia is a very dark forest with many hungry wolves in it. And Gorbachov, he is the worst wolf of them all."

Lucy managed to get them a room in Babushkinskaya, a northern suburb. "Watch out when you come out of the subway. Moscow is full of young *malchyks* robbing and beating up tourists like you."

On the subway, nobody talked, all faces frozen stiff from *Dyed Maroz*, Grandpa Frosty, or some other Soviet terror. A people full of dignity, except for the biting reek of unwashed armpits. Deodorant was pure luxury. When they got off, a young man was walking alongside them up to the street level. Here it was pitch dark already. He was an interpreter of French and worked for the Ministry of the Interior. "Look," he said, "I'm a good husband. I'm bringing my wife some flowers. We got married two months ago." He told them proudly that he made five hundred *roubli* on his new job. The average monthly salary in

Moscow was around three hundred. "Your wife must be proud of you," said Alice. He blushed.

"Can you live off five hundred?"

"Of course. An apartment costs ten *roubli* a month unless you want something a little more *privé*, something a little more deluxe. We'll probably get such an apartment soon, since I work for the government now."

Jonathan asked him why there were so many beggars in Moscow. They were everywhere in devout position holding out their shapkas, their eyes averted.

"They earn a lot more than anyone else," he said. "About three hundred *roubli* a day. People are embarrassed that socialism has produced beggars, so they give them plenty to get them off the streets."

The satellite town of Babushkinskaya was a gigantic Christmas tree, its thousands of lit-up windows in the cold night. With ten *roubli*, around thirty US cents, the landlady earned one month's worth of rent per night. A sort of capitalism within socialism. She talked incessantly but was exceptionally friendly, unlike most other Russian women, he thought, who had been screaming at them, especially him. So far, only one of them had laughed, that was upon their arrival in Moscow, at the train station restaurant, where as usual there was nothing to eat. Alice wanted an egg, and he had to translate, but the word for egg escaped him since the eggs themselves had been escaping them for such a long time now. Even the phrase book wasn't handy, so Jonathan just stood up from the table and started cackling like a chicken while pointing his index at his butt. The waitress understood immediately and laughed like he had not heard anyone laugh since the Sydney days. They heard her laugh for a full twenty minutes back in the kitchen, and she was still laughing when she came back with tea, laughing, cackling, and saying *Nyet*. For even in Moscow there were no eggs. There was less food in Moscow than on the train.

Wherever they went, they came across people lining up outside of the empty stores. All poverty withstanding, these shops contained a beautifully elaborate interior design but not a crumb on all those silver trays. His mood was rapidly deteriorating. Since their last meal with Alexej and Vadim, they hadn't eaten anything but Lucy's lemon drops. Even their landlady in Babushkinskaya had nothing but tea. McDonald's was the only place selling food, as all of Moscow knew. The queue wound around a park before going down almost the entire length of Gorski Prospekt. Eating here meant taking a day off. Lining up early in the morning, hours before they even opened. Jonathan and Alice walked to the end of the line, where they spotted Martin and his new-age girlfriend. He was more composed than he'd been outside of the Russian embassy in Beijing, maybe because he knew he was close to home. At the very end of the line stood a young giantess towering over him by the full length of a head. A Russian Alice.

"Should we get some food here," he asked Alice who had moved on already.

"To tell you the truth," she said, "I'd rather starve than eat American fast food in Russia."

She looked at him earnestly.

"Was there anything of interest back there?"

"Why, what d'you mean?"

"I thought for a moment I saw you looking at that Russian Amazon. You were glazing over."

"It's true. I did look at her."

She came closer and leaning onto her crutches looked him straight in the eyes.

"You like 'em tall, don't you?"

Her eyes were full of that tenderness that he remembered so well from their first encounter all those years ago. He'd carried that gaze of hers with him wherever he went—it was like a small treasure. They stood kissing for a long while on Gorski Prospekt, half-starved and with Russia all around them on the brink of collapse.

Everywhere there were signs of change. The best of the West catching up. Baskin-Robbins: a sundae for thirteen dollars. In front of it Yuri Long-arm, the founder of Moscow, was surrounded by a group of youths with blue-white-red flags.

"What's going on?"

"We're Russians," one of the young guys said, "we want to get out of the Union." Arbatskaya Street was full of stalls selling Russian artifacts: jewel boxes, hats, and *matryoshka* dolls, those wooden puppets without hands. Around six or more nest inside the mother doll. The smallest one is about as big as a grape and can no longer be opened by her waist. As Jonathan rolled one of them over in his palm, he was thinking of the trip nearing its end here in Moscow. A journey made up of concentric rings: the outer one, from Germany to Australia and back, then, going further inward, the circle around Australia, even further within, from Alice Springs to Uluru and back again, and then the smallest nested doll within all the others – was it perhaps his swim through the dark waters of Ellery Creek, over to the beach between the two cliffs and back again? It had felt like swimming to some origin, from there back into the world again.

Another train. Moscow – Warsaw. Finally, someone was feeding them again, a chatty Ukrainian woman with an unending supply of salami sandwiches. The only word he understood from her—she kept using it with a certain probing, questioning expression on her face—was *visa*. Did she want to know how many Ukrainian salami sandwiches it took to get an invitation into the West? Unfortunately, neither he nor Alice managed to eat more than two of her door-step-sized sandwiches. Their stomachs had shrunk badly over the last weeks. She was very disappointed that he in particular ate so little, eyeing him unhappily the way the witch does Hänsel. The other compartment passenger was an impeccably dressed Armenian with so many bags and packages that one was tempted to think he wanted to open a market in Poland. At the border, he was seized by violent attacks of nervousness. He kept looking around as if he were being hunted, talking to some shady characters on the platform. Suddenly he started handing all his luggage through the window, all the bags and packages, except one.

Then he disappeared.

The militia was walking through the train collecting entry forms. One of the immigration officers spotted the Armenian's bag, asked the Ukrainian something, they started yelling at each other, then he left.

Silence.

The wait at the Russian-Polish border lasted several hours, as the train was being searched over and over, mirrors were being driven below its underside, and uniformed men pounded on its walls with crowbars, like physicians using little hammers on their patients to find out if their bodies contained foreign objects. Finally, someone blew a whistle. The train started moving slowly through desolate no-man's-land, then picked up speed again.

Just before Warsaw a *provodnik* yelled at them for the last time. It was to be a lasting memory: the yelling women of Russia. The proximity of the West gave him wings and he yelled back at her.

"Why are you screaming at us? We don't understand Russian and no matter how loud you get it won't be clearer to us."

Instantly, she fell silent and looked at him dumbfounded, almost intimidated, as if she wanted to say: I don't mean to be rude to you, we, the women of Russia, have to yell all the time or our stubborn men won't function. Her stern face suddenly collapsed, her heavy features breaking into an almost servile smile.

Warsaw was a city belonging to the West. Some of its neighborhoods looked like Rothenburg ob der Tauber, one of Germany's prettiest towns. The days of starving were over, although Jonathan was as good as broke. Alice seemed to have an endless supply of cash, but he did not want to freeload on her. He had forty US dollars left, twenty of which he exchanged in the black market. There were opportunities for this almost everywhere. For twenty dollars the bank would have given him a hundred thousand słoty, but the two young men outside a small grocery store promised ten thousand more. One of them started counting the bills into Jonathan's hand, a hundred thousand słoty bill, then ten thousand, then one two three four five six seven eight nine thousand, whoops, wait a minute, one bill was missing, he started counting again, took all the bills back, palm empty again, and started putting them back on, all the way to the last słoty bill. You're an honest man, Jonathan tells him, but they're already gone. He counts again, but where the hell was the hundred thousand słoty bill that guy had put down first, there were only twenty thousand.

It was a finger trick. More than half a year on the road and then only a day from home, to be robbed for the first time. His mood was darkening. Twenty thousand słoty, a little over four dollars, and only twenty bucks in his pocket.

Those too stayed in Poland.

To save money, he dodged the tram fare. Promptly, they were caught. By two very young plainclothes conductors showing their identity cards and asking for two hundred thousand słoty. Do a runner? With Alice on crutches?

"Ha," he snorted, "anyone can do this, get some piece of cardboard with Polish on it, stick a photo to it and try to rake in two hundred thousand słoty."

"You're questioning our identity," one of the young Poles replied in excellent German, "why don't we go to the police and sort it out there?"

A good idea.

Their IDs were perfectly legit. Jonathan handed over his last twenty dollars, showing them his empty wallet to prove they'd cleaned him out. He was absolutely broke now. "Well," the Pole said, "you're from the West. You can afford it."

He heard himself growling like a wounded animal. That they were not coming from the West but that they had been traveling for months, through China and Siberia, that this was his last money that he had just taken from him, and that he had been on the road for almost a year, that they had traveled through the Australian outback, and that even Westerners did run out of money at some point.

The eyes of the young Pole were widening more and more as the synopsis of their travels unfolded. When Jonathan mentioned Australia, he recognized in the young Pole that old familiar glimmer of yearning mixed with awe that he had seen so often in people far away from down under.

"You were in Australia? Do you still have coins from all those countries you've gone through?"

They started digging around in their backpacks again, and sure enough, there were a few forgotten yuan, and even a golden Australian dollar skipped into Alice's hand. As Jonathan looked at it, a pang of longing hit him briefly, but they gave their treasures to the Pole to please his numismatic penchant. The young man was as happy as a child at Christmas. He shook hands with them most heartily, reiterating how sorry he was about the twenty dollars he just had to take from him for having no ticket.

"It doesn't matter," Alice reassured him, "what's most important is that Poland, Germany, and Australia are at peace again."

She paid for the tickets from Warsaw to Hanover. Somewhere in western Poland she said: "Around here must've been where they pulled Uncle Wolfram off the train to Auschwitz."

It was strange, her uncle's work in Theresienstadt, and how it saved him from being deported to Auschwitz. Having to treat his enemy's illnesses. The camp disguised as a spa resort for the purpose of demonstrating to the world that genocide was not happening. And yet, something very similar had happened in his own hometown, the *Kurort* of his childhood, where, he remembered, people were talking about how the local bath houses that were generally used for therapy had, after the war, been turned into interrogation centers by the Allied Forces, and how they were torturing German prisoners there who were suspected of being Communist spies.

Perpetrators and victims, the line wasn't always clear. In the camps, he remembered his teacher Grummler telling them, there had been *Kapos*, victims working for the perpetrators, by which they were able to prolong their survival.

In a way, he dreaded going back to his origins, but then, as he stepped in front of the window and the train was moving across the border into Frankfurt an der Oder, a part of Germany he'd never seen before, receiving him back into the *Vater- und Mutterland*, a strange warm feeling stirred in his heart.

All of a sudden, a bulky shadow emerged out of nowhere. Blonde moustache, steel blue eyes. In his green uniform he positioned himself right in front of Alice, looking up at her.

"*Was ist das?*" he asked, pointing at her as if he were looking at a strange animal trying to crawl across his threshold.

"I'm Australian."

Her answer did not have the power to de-petrify the immigration officer, it merely caused him to flick his fingers, his way of asking to see her passport.

It was half an hour to East Berlin.

Gray façades in brilliant sunshine. Some people seemed serene. Modest, helpful, full of optimism. At the ticket machine: Berlin Zoo— two marks for East Germans, two marks seventy for Westerners. The wall was porous, the parliament building towering in the milky glare of light.

They weren't used to it any more. The so-called West. Test the West.

Everything was so clean and all around them the dour faces of those who have it all.

Finally, too, there was toilet paper again.

How they were staring at her! Some made a wide berth around her. This staring was not like the Chinese stares of curiosity. It was of a more aggressive nature, it contained a promise of violence, but violence that failed to release itself thanks to its brother, cowardice.

Alice was surprised: "Why are they staring like this? Is it these old-fashioned crutches?"

"Probably," he said. "They're thinking: she looks foreign, she's a cripple, and she probably expects us to feed her."

They got on the train from Berlin to Hanover. From East to West to East to West again.

The majority of travelers were stern and silent men reading the economics pages on their way to work. An old woman, a Jehovah's Witness, was trying to sell Alice the only true faith in life. She admired Jonathan's strength, the woman said. That he didn't attempt to touch Alice, kiss her, not even to hold her hand: it proved to her, she said, that he was saving himself for her. He was beginning to understand the silent newspaper readers: the only way not to be bothered by others was to hide behind a paper.

Still *biriosa*. Rusty Trabant cars, called Trabis, in birch tree groves outside factory ruins. The East lay fallow, waiting to be fertilized by Western values. Soon after Magdeburg, they crossed the German-German border, a brown freshly plowed field, and in the middle of it a fence losing itself on the horizon like those telegraph poles in Siberia so many miles ago. Then, once again, neat Western houses fully equipped with red roofs, VW Rabbits parked outside the garage, and skateboarding kids on solid sidewalks.

A short stop in Braunschweig: Wilhelm Raabe spent most of his life here, and it was the place Gerstäcker sometimes returned to, to see his mother and the wife he had left behind during his travels. He pulled the biography from his pack and started reading to Alice.

*There he was again one day, having traversed the deserts of Egypt, the jungles of Latin America, the prairies of North America, the pampas of Argentina, having walked the cordilleras in the winter, and sailed to the islands in the South Pacific. Home eluded him, and he liked it that way. No matter where he was, he always wanted to be somewhere else. As soon as he was back in Germany, his insatiable wanderlust would drive him forth into the world again. He loathed living among the philistines, as nineteenth-century German writers called the rising middle class seeking comfort and turning away from politics. An attitude he shared with Heinrich Heine. But then again, running through the world like a stray dog, he kept being haunted by unbearable homesickness, tormented by an irrepressible yearning for the distant roots of his childhood, while cultivating his wild penchant for the peripheral corners of the globe. Forever torn between* Heimweh *and* Fernweh, *homesickness and a yearning for faraway places—did they not grow from the same seed? Tormented by nostalgia in the true sense of the word: the pain for the lost home he returned to Germany. There he was again one day after his journey round the world, walking into Braunschweig, only to find out that his wife had not waited for him, for she had died in the meantime.*

Hanover Central: those old, now almost unfamiliar, sounds of North German uncouthness. The smell of urine wafting from the underground shopping passage and the usual slouch-shouldered unemployed men in their mid-thirties schlepping themselves and their cans of Herforder Pils to the sausage stalls outside the station.

A regional train takes them out to his hometown. The train stops and throws him back into the small world of his childhood.

Not quite.

He had traveled the world and the world had traveled him. Surely, he must have outgrown this place and its people. His backpack and the windswept apparition he'd become, his transformed body and soul, were abundant proof of that. This muted atmosphere of a German spa town—with its dubious Sunday concerts, its meticulous sense of orderliness, its pastry shops selling pralines reminiscent of digestive refuse but with the promising name of spa mud, its drinking water smelling of foul eggs, its steaming thermal baths where athlete's foot slumbers, and its deadly stillness in the early afternoon, a stillness decreed by the spa police—all this could no longer get to him. The mere memory of it used to make him want to choke and chunder, but now, finally, he was beyond all this.

Approaching his parents' small row house, he saw some kids shooting a soccer ball at an open garage door. He wanted to walk up to them and yell at them: listen kids, if you're as freedom loving as I am, do as I have done, leave this place some day and follow your dreams and yearnings, don't look back. Run! Run to the distant horizons of this world.

"There'll be a day when we don't travel like this anymore," said Alice.

"What do you mean?"

"You know, all these adventures, chance encounters with strange people, hitchhiking and not knowing if anyone will pick you up."

"You think one day this will be a lost art?"

She looked at him and smiled. "The lost beauty of happenstance."

"Boy. Look at you. How skinny you are!" Mom and Dad were shaking hands with him. They always shook hands, no matter how long and far he had been away. They also shook hands with Alice. Looking up at her, they moved together a bit and stood stock-still.

To Jonathan's surprise, his father looked quite healthy. His skin was leathery and tanned, and he had lost some weight.

"You look well."

He gave his son a wan smile.

"Don't let looks fool you."

Mom soon disappeared into the basement from where he heard the familiar howl of the laundry machine. It was a small world. But wherever the train stops, wherever you get off, the world becomes small sooner or later, and won't widen again until you're back on the tracks.

He was sick for a week, his mother and Alice competing to play a role in his recovery. Every time Alice left the house, Mom was yelling a lot over the phone to Dad who was working away in the pharmacy. Alice's presence was problematic. To bring a guest home was always difficult. Clean bed sheets had to be taken out of the closet and a guest wanted to use the bathroom every now and then. Alice was used to taking a shower twice a day, especially now that they were no longer on the Russian train. Little did she know that her craving for personal hygiene conflicted with Mom's obsession with orderliness. This obsession tended to make her lose all civility. Mother, as host, was downright hostile. Every time Alice stepped out of the bathroom, she would run in to open the window—so the steam could escape—and to inspect the shower. As the product of her upbringing, Jonathan was used to being careful to clean the shower as scrupulously as possible, ridding the drainage of all real and imagined hair, and using the windscreen-wiper-type device to erase the trace of all water drops from the white ceramic-tiled walls. Still, he had never succeeded in leaving the bathroom in such a state that it would not disturb the domestic sensitivities of his mother. So how could one expect Alice, who came from the free world where people were allowed to be casual, where hospitality mattered more than a perfect domestic order, how could she be expected to know that she was bound to fall into this cultural trap? Even if he'd warned her, these things could not be explained. She would have had to grow up with it to understand.

"The whole bathroom was underwater again," Mom complained to Dad after a week had gone by since their son's arrival. She was hoping that he would side with her, which he usually did, for normally he would say:

"Do you have to cause your Mom so much work?" or "Can you not be a little more careful with these things? It all costs so much money."

Usually, when he made these statements, he'd use the second person plural, thereby also addressing his daughter. But she was no longer present. She had moved out many years ago. And Dad did not say anything this time. It was strange, but he'd become abnormally quiet during his son's absence. All his cynicism seemed to have vanished.

A few days after his return, he told Alice he needed to visit Grandma Ilse, Mom and Uncle Rudi's mother. Before he left for Australia, she used to visit his parents for dinner, possibly because she wanted to see more of her daughter—she was approaching a hundred years of age—but maybe also because she had just canceled her meals on wheels service.

"Two fifty a day, don't you think that's theft?" she'd complained. Mom and Dad were worried, of course, that she might starve to death.

"Don't worry about it, Ursel," she said, tapping her daughter's lower arm: "every day the neighbor leaves a plate full of food outside my door. Her husband Wilhelm can't eat all that grub with his rotten stomach. He hasn't been himself since the last war. Every time the fire truck goes by, he almost has a heart attack. Those sirens remind him of the air raids, he says, and all the nights we spent together in the bunkers."

Grandma Ilse's parsimony was a virtue that had accompanied her all through life, but it was increasing with age. Her weekly exercise consisted in walking to the bank to ask the tellers to write down her balance. The bank clerks had nicknamed her *Festgeld Ilse*, "Interest Ilse."

She recycled everything. When they were children, he remembered, she would wash Grandpa's condoms after he'd used them, and slip them on to the round brass knobs of her doors like bank robber masks. It slowed down their wear and tear, and saved her from having to waste polish to clean away finger prints.

Grandpa Ferdinand had died a long time ago, but not before passing on some of his wisdom to his grandchildren. His favorite meal was potatoes with brown gravy. He would mush it all up on his plate until his potato nuggets had turned into mashed potatoes, and the gravy was completely and evenly distributed in the mash, displaying an evenly brown consistency. It was not until this had been achieved that he would lean over his plate to relish the pulp in small forkfuls. Again and again, he would warn his grandchildren against the big mouthfuls and greedy gulps from the cold apple juice. "Don't put too much into your mouth," he would say, "Take small bites and small gulps so you don't ruin your stomach."

Grandma Ilse didn't own a dishwasher. She did not need one, since Grandpa would always eat his plate clean. Then he would hold it close to his face and lick criss and cross, up and down, and back and forth over it until it looked brand new. Grandma Ilse would then wipe her kitchen towel across it once or twice before placing it back in the cupboard where it would wait patiently for the next potato-and-gravy meal. It saved her having to waste water and dish soap.

Opa Ferdinand spent all his days sitting on the green wooden box in the kitchen smoking his cigar and reading the local paper, the *Hannoversche Allgemeine*. The box had been kept tightly locked to this day. Jonathan had never had the courage to break it open. Ferdinand never spoke much, except when the kids got too loud, then he would growl a short "be quiet now," and when they still kept up their ruckus he would, giant that he was, stand up from his box, almost scraping the ceiling with his head. He seized the bamboo stick from on top of the kitchen cupboard, sliced the air with it and whipped the kitchen table at which they were sitting, shocking them into silence.

He left the house only to sit in his favorite spot at the far end of the large garden, between the shed with its smell of wet earth and the cherry tree that was cut down one day because its branches had become so long that they hung low into the neighbor's yard. Shortly after the war there was a deep pit next to this tree where a bomb had struck the ground, without damaging the house. Mother used to play in it when she was a child.

Sometimes he would talk about the French. He insisted on calling them *Franzmänner*, Frenchies. It was the Frenchies who'd destroyed his legs in the First World War and made him limp for the rest of his life. When they were kids he wanted to hear that story again and again, of how Grandpa and his buddies were standing in a circle when a hand grenade struck right in the middle of them. Nobody survived except Ferdinand who was immediately taken to hospital because of the shrapnel in his torn legs. There he fell in love with his nurse and never had to go back to the front. "Let's not talk about that," he would say when he had got to the part of the story in which the nurse appeared, "Ilse doesn't want to hear about this."

Once, Jonathan remembered, walking through their apartment, he found his Opa's war journal. It was hidden in the bookshelf between the cigar box containing his swastika party badges, a small silver whistle, and Hitler's *Mein Kampf*, a book Opa hid in the bomb pit under the cherry tree at the end of the Second World War and did not dig up again until the 1950s. His handwriting was hard to decipher but Jonathan could never forget one entry that he managed to figure out. It was only one line but aptly described the mentality of a soldier who understood his presence at the front as his profession. It said:

*Heute war ein guter Tag—Flasche Rotwein getrunken und zwei Franzmänner um die Ecke gebracht.* Today was a good day—drank a bottle of red wine and finished off two Frenchies.

*Um die Ecke gebracht:* literally it meant he had brought the Frenchies round the corner, the corner that led from life to death. Jonathan had often asked himself in what order this may have happened. Had his Opa drunk the bottle of red wine first, before killing the Frenchmen? Or had he killed them, and then drunk the wine? The timing was an important detail, since it revealed different motivations. Had he used the red wine to muster courage for the killing, to celebrate it, or to forget about it? He never asked him when he was alive. Nor did he ask him about the Nazis, about whom he never talked anyway.

The years before he died, Ferdinand spent most of his time in bed simply staring at the wall. His vision had become so weak that he could no longer read the *Hannoversche Allgemeine*, and a cyst next to his right eye had grown to such proportions that it covered the eye almost completely. His feet were aching even when he sat on the large wooden box in the kitchen. He was always on his guard with Grandma Ilse, for she was keen on popping the cyst. She wanted to cut it open so that the gunk would ooze out and improve his eye-sight. She was also haunted by the suspicion that he had become so senile that he would not remember the people closest to him, not even his own relatives. One day she put him to the test.

"Who is this?" she said when Dad had walked in to see how he was doing. Grandpa Ferdinand opened his tired eyes and gave his son-in-law a long and forlorn stare.

"Adolf," he said and closed his lids again.

In great despair, Grandma Ilse ran out of the bed room and yelled: "For heaven's sake. His arse will snap shut any day now." It was her way of saying that he would die soon. As soon as she was out the door Opa winked at Dad with his healthy eye:

"She's a little nuts, you know. Of course, I know it's you, Ulli."

A few days later though, his arse did snap shut.

Ever since then, Ilse had been living in a local retirement home.

She wasn't happy with the decision.

Within a short time, she managed to make herself very unpopu-lar. "We had to separate her from the others," said one of the nurses, "after she broke someone's shin bone with her cane." The old man had made himself feel a little too much at home on the sofa in one of the impeccably polished corridors. He had stretched out his legs a little too far at the very moment when Deposit Ilse was marching by him. In a high arc, like a golf club, she swung her cane and deposited it as hard as she could on the poor guy's lower leg, which was brittle with the calcium deficiency typical of his age. Apparently, it broke like a dry twig.

While Mom hardly ever visited her, Dad came by almost every day bringing her cookies and flowers, patiently listening to the volley of abuse with which she repaid his kindness.

"I'd prefer to eat green soap," she said to Jonathan when he and Alice were visiting her, "to seeing your Dad." Her hatred of his father was completely irrational.

"I wouldn't mind bashing his face in with my cane," she said.

She was staring hard at Alice, her olive skin in particular, then leaned forward to him and said: "Me boy, are they all that yellow in Australia?"

* * *

The next day Alice was gone.

The night before Mom had been talking about various friends and acquaintances of his, what they were up to, how they had started careers and were already making a pile of cash. She mentioned Manfred, the butcher's son who used to be his archenemy and had tried to beat him up under the arching tree on that day so many years ago when Alice saved him.

"You know what," Mom said. "That butcher boy, Manfred, he died."

He was speechless.

"Yes. He lived in Berlin and jumped from the fifth floor of the hospital and broke his spine. He lived another five hours but they couldn't save him. When the police went to his parents' house they said: We're sorry, but your son died this morning. He committed suicide, they said. He had AIDS. They didn't have a clue. Their son had never told them. He'd never told them he was gay either. Can you imagine? One day the police just turn up at your doorstep and tell you your son is dead, committed suicide because he had AIDS, and he had AIDS because he was gay, and they didn't know about any of it. Apparently, the psychiatrist in hospital had told him to talk to his parents as he was getting worse. But he just couldn't tell them, especially his father."

Alice had gone as white as a sheet. Suddenly she got up, grabbed her crutches and excused herself.

"Doesn't it bother you that she's like that?" Mom said after Alice had left the room. She could be very jumpy in her thoughts. "You can't be serious about her. No wonder her knees don't function, with those weird proportions."

"What do you mean? Weird proportions?!" he snapped. "She had an accident on the Great Wall of China."

His father just sat there and remained quiet.

Outside he could hear the stairway creak its old melody, singing of someone going cautiously upstairs. His parents had heard it too. Mom did not say another word.

He was upset and soon retired to his basement room, crawled into his childhood bed. As he turned to switch off the light he spotted those letters again he had once carved into the bedhead: BURY ME IN AUSTRALIA. They were still legible. Well, it was too late for that. Germans die first out there, but he'd been one of the lucky few who had escaped.

He woke again to an incredible din. Where the heck was he? He looked around him and suddenly it dawned on him again: the basement of his parental home in North Germany, the incredible noise and nagging came from his mother on the phone, where she spent much of her time. Day after day she was fighting clamorous battles with useless handymen, impudent neighbors, lazy city functionaries, or Granny Ilse. The problems were for the most part of a serious nature: the neighbor's dachshund had barked again during the municipally imposed early-afternoon time of rest; the speeders had not slowed down again, endangering the lives of the children who should not be playing near the street anyway. The huge rumbling basement oil tank was leaking again, or the cleaning woman who came by twice a week needed to be fired for incompetence, for once again a grain of dirt had escaped her, probably for the simple reason that in their house no grain of dirt could ever be detected by the human eye.

"*Die sind wir wohl los.* I guess we got rid of her." Almost screaming, Mom broke into his basement cave, opening the windows to let out the cloud of nocturnal decomposition.

"*Die sind wir wohl los,*" she repeated. "That's a great friendship, wouldn't you say?"

His health was completely restored by then. The fever was gone, his limbs no longer aching.

"By the way, she left this here for you." Mom put the note right next to his plate loaded with the *Wurst* sandwiches and the obligatory four apple quarters he had been getting from her since the days his memory had first started kicking in.

*Dear Jonathan, couldn't hack it anymore. I think you know where to find me. Love, A.*

He was hopping mad. Mom pretended not to listen. It was cleaning day, like every Monday, Wednesday, and Friday. All doors and windows stood wide open, although it was still freezing cold outside. The new cleaning woman was there too. The two women were schlepping the heavy Persian rugs into the yard, where they started pummeling them with carpet beaters that looked like elongated tennis rackets. They kept beating away, committing dust-mite murder and to announce to the whole neighborhood what orderly and upstanding *Hausfrauen* they were. Then they dragged the carpets back inside, rolled them out and began crawling on all fours round their periphery, both of them straightening out the fringes with combs.

His father was generally annoyed by the loss of *Gemütlichkeit* resulting from this ritual with the rugs, but of course he knew that housecleaning, especially in the spring, was inevitable. Dad had never helped Mom and her cleaning women carry the heavy Persians carpets. Under their weight, he would no doubt have collapsed. He just sat there staring at the display of matriarchal vigor unfolding in front of him.

Watching these familiar patterns, Jonathan bit into a *Wurst* sandwich. He knew he should really offer to help, but he also knew that Mom wouldn't let him. She had grown up in postwar rubble, had witnessed how the women cleaned up Germany—they were the so-called *Trümmerfrauen*, women who handled the mess on their own because the guys weren't around, most of them dead from the war or not returning from it until much later.

Raw minced beef. Steak tartare. His appetite had come back and the days of parting the tiger were over. His acne had come back too, and with a vengeance. It had completely disappeared while he was still traveling. Germany, *Heimat*, home sweet home. It always made him break out.

He got up and broke free.

I think you know where to find me, she had said on the note. He had no idea. He ran over to the train station. But nobody had seen a tall young woman on crutches. Then he went to the house where he and

Alice had first kissed, and rang the bell. Uncle Wolfram opened, and there was Alice's mother standing in the corridor. Jonathan didn't have to say anything. "Try the park," she said. "You'll find her there."

On the way to the park, he bought a piece of *Baumkuchen* to go, his favorite kind of cake.

Looking at its shape, the chocolate arch, it dawned on him where exactly Alice could have gone. Had he not told her once that, whenever he was in distress, he'd always run up to his favorite tree, his island of beauty and harmony at the top of the park?

He could already see it from a distance. Its gentle arch from one end to the other, allowing you to climb over it, moving slowly along while sitting and wrapping your legs around its trunk. He realized now it was a symbol of migration from one world to another, a symbol of bridging all partitions and distances—the present and the past. Back then, it had just been a way to climb away from this little town, to rise above all the pettiness.

Alice was sitting right at the top, her back turned to him. For a moment he expected her to morph into that supernatural being Ludwig Tieck described in his novella, the forest woman Christian encounters when he runs off for the last time to the mountains in search of his beautiful giantess. But instead of finding the gorgeous woman he had seen there during his earlier journey, he encounters the *Waldweib*, the witch who drives him to madness. That entirely male projection stemming from a deeply patriarchal world: Venus in the mountain, woman of the forest, beautiful to behold as long as she faces the male gaze. The moment she turns around, however, she morphs into a hollow tree with nothing but rough bark hanging from her. But Alice was still his Alice. Or was she not?

"Are you OK?"

She didn't say anything. She just kept staring ahead at the hills to the south. Suffused by forest they were shrouded in mist. There were no leaves on any of the trees. Her crutches were leaning against the upended root, which looked like the mane of a giant creature. As a young boy, he had often been terrified by these scraggly roots that could be found all over the Deister hills, where his father, sister, and he would go hiking off beaten paths on Sunday afternoons.

He climbed up to her, sat by her side, and slipped his arm around her waist.

For a long time they didn't speak.

It was Alice who broke the silence.

"You see those hills over there?"

"The Deister Range."

"Yes, the Deister. About half way between here and Hamelin, that's where the mineshaft is that Mom was hiding in during the war."

"Is this why you came up here?"

Alice turned around and looked at him with an intensity he'd never seen on her.

"The past has a way of repeating itself," she said after a pause. What was that word about working through the past that your teacher taught us back then, *Vergangenheit* something or other?"

"*Vergangenheitsbewältigung.*"

"That's it. Working through the past, acting out and working through it so the soul can heal. Well, in Mom's case, she's still working through things."

"What do you mean?"

"She was raped in the final days of the war. She told me this morning."

He stared at her, she was staring at the hills to the south.

"You mean: over there?"

"Yes, over there. It happened in the mine, where she was meant to be protected from evil. This was the main reason why Mom left Germany and never wanted to return. You can imagine how nervous she must have been when she sent me over here eleven years ago to attend the very school she used to go to as a child. But I suppose she had hoped for some sort of reconciliation with her native country, some sort of healing through me and my generation."

"Who raped her?"

"The man we always thought of as our friend."

"Hermann?"

"Yes. Hermann."

"And your uncle? Did he not know?"

"He did. But never did anything about it, because he owed his own life to Hermann. It's crazy, isn't it, to be torn all your life between gratitude and accusation."

She was staring into the landscape. He remembered the entrance of one of the mines. When he was a child his father had taken him there on several occasions. It was blocked off by an iron gate with a big rusty lock on it. Behind it gaped a black hole. It was breathing cold damp air at you and he could see his own breath being swallowed by it, even in the summer.

"Coward." She spat out the word. "He never defended me either."

"What do you mean?"

"Do you remember how I left the weekend after you and I were up here, and we had that run-in with that butcher's son, Manfred?"

"I do. I . . . nobody in class understood why you left."

"You remember how we went to the café, how we were hiding from him. I'd lost my wallet, it had slipped out as I was helping you off this tree. From this very spot where we're now sitting. I came back up here the next day looking for it. Found it immediately, it was just down there in the middle of the path."

Alice looked at the Deister again. The mist had been lifting a little, the spring sun trying to work its way through to touch the barren trees.

"When I bent to pick it up I was thrown to the ground and dragged over there, behind those roots."

"Thrown over? Dragged? What! I don't understand."

"Manfred."

"Manfred?"

"Yes. Manfred. He must have known that I would come back here to look for it. He must have found it when he got off the tree after we ran away. And he came back, planted it here, and waited for me. He was waiting behind those roots. To attack me. Like some wild animal of the woods."

Her expression had gone blank, stony.

The fog over the southern hills had almost completely disappeared.

"Did he—?"

She stared at the ground below.

"He had such terrible strength in him. I tried to kick him between the legs, but it didn't stop him."

An elderly couple was passing underneath them, their dachshund on a short leash, sniffing the ground. They were dressed in loden, he with a green hunter's hat, a trophy feather sticking from it. They both fell silent until the couple had passed on.

"Did you tell your uncle what Manfred did to you?"

"Yes."

"And? Did he not go after him? Or his family?!"

"No. He immediately sent me back to Australia. Kept it all quiet. I'm sure it's because he didn't want to lose his patients. It's a small town. Accusing the son of a local business man . . . it might have been bad for his own business."

"Are you going to contact his family?"

"What? Manfred's family?"

"Yes."

"After all these years?"

"Sure. I don't think there is an expiry date on things like this."

She hesitated.

"I don't know," she said. "Manfred's dead now. His parents must be hurting bad enough. What good would it do to add to their grief?"

"But what about you? Wouldn't it help you to come to terms with it?"

"You mean, my very own *Vergangenheitsbewältigung*? I've never liked that word, you know, it's too close to that other one, the one for rape, *vergewaltigen*. Acting out and working through. Tell me: How do you act out being raped? Anyway, the one thing I know is that my uncle still needs to answer for his silence about what happened to my mother. And to me."

Jonathan didn't know how to respond. His eyes wandered along the arch of the tree to where it branched out into a warren of boughs thinning into twigs. A red squirrel had been watching them intently, nibbling away at some beech nut or acorn, its bushy tail quivering slightly.

"Let me show you something," he said after a prolonged silence.

He took her hand in his, placing her palm against the tree, stretching out their intertwined fingers over a spot in the bark.

"What is it?" she asked as her fingertips grazed the wood.

"Try to make it out."

Her fingers were moving gently under his touch.

"It's an old carving," she said, slowly, her smile spreading as her nail followed the faint grooves of J + A inside a deeply hewn heart. Years of moss had turned it green.

**Peter Arnds** is the Director of Comparative Literature and Head of Italian at Trinity College Dublin. A native of Germany, he has also lived in Kansas, Kabul, and Delhi. He is a member of PEN and has just finished his second novel, *Detachment*. He is currently working on a collection of short stories entitled *The Lost Beauty of Happenstance*.

# Selected Dalkey Archive Paperbacks

Michal Ajvaz, *Empty Streets*
  *Journey to the South*
  *The Golden Age*
  *The Other City*
David Albahari, *Gotz & Meyer*
  *Learning Cyrillic*
Pierre Albert-Birot, *The First Book of Grabinoulor*
Svetlana Alexievich, *Voices from Chernobyl*
Felipe Alfau, *Chromos*
  *Locos*
João Almino, *Enigmas of Spring*
  *Free City*
  *The Book of Emotions*
Ivan Ângelo, *The Celebration*
David Antin, *Talking*
Djuna Barnes, *Ladies Almanack*
  *Ryder*
John Barth, *The End of the Road*
  *The Floating Opera*
  *The Tidewater Tales*
Donald Barthelme, *Paradise*
  *The King*
Svetislav Basara, *Chinese Letter*
  *Fata Morgana*
  *The Mongolian Travel Guide*
Andrej Blatnik, *Law of Desire*
  *You Do Understand*
Patrick Bolshauser, *Rapids*
Louis Paul Boon, *Chapel Road*
  *My Little War*
  *Summer in Termuren*
Roger Boylan, *Killoyle*
Ignacio de Loyola Brandão, *And Still the Earth*
  *Anonymous Celebrity*
  *The Good-Bye Angel*
Sébastien Brebel, *Francis Bacon's Armchair*
Christine Brooke-Rose, *Amalgamemnon*
Brigid Brophy, *In Transit*
  *Prancing Novelist: In Praise of Ronald Firbank*
Gerald L. Bruns, *Modern Poetry and the Idea of Language*
Lasha Bugadze, *The Literature Express*
Dror Burstein, *Kin*
Michel Butor, *Mobile*
Julieta Campos, *The Fear of Losing Eurydice*
Anne Carson, *Eros the Bittersweet*
Camilo José Cela, *Family of Pascual Duarte*
Louis-Ferdinand Céline, *Castle to Castle*
Hugo Charteris, *The Tide Is Right*
Luis Chitarroni, *The No Variations*
Jack Cox, *Dodge Rose*
Ralph Cusack, *Cadenza*
Stanley Crawford, *Log of the S.S. the Mrs. Unguentine*
  *Some Instructions to My Wife*
Robert Creeley, *Collected Prose*
Nicholas Delbanco, *Sherbrookes*
Rikki Ducornet, *The Complete Butcher's Tales*
William Eastlake, *Castle Keep*
Stanley Elkin, *The Dick Gibson Show*
  *The Magic Kingdom*
Gustave Flaubert, *Bouvard et Pécuchet*
Jon Fosse, *Melancholy I*
  *Melancholy II*
  *Trilogy*
Max Frisch, *I'm Not Stiller*
  *Man in the Holocene*
Carlos Fuentes, *Christopher Unborn*
  *Great Latin American Novel*
  *Nietzsche on His Balcony*
  *Terra Nostra*
  *Where the Air Is Clear*
William Gaddis, *J R*
  *The Recognitions*

William H. Gass, *A Temple of Texts*
  *Cartesian Sonata and Other Novellas*
  *Finding a Form*
  *Life Sentences*
  *Reading Rilke*
  *Tests of Time: Essays*
  *The Tunnel*
  *Willie Masters' Lonesome Wife*
  *World Within the Word*
Etienne Gilson, *Forms and Substances in the Arts*
  *The Arts of the Beautiful*
Douglas Glover, *Bad News of the Heart*
Paulo Emílio Sales Gomes, *P's Three Women*
Juan Goytisolo, *Count Julian*
  *Juan the Landless*
  *Marks of Identity*
Alasdair Gray, *Poor Things*
Jack Green, *Fire the Bastards!*
Jiří Gruša, *The Questionnaire*
Mela Hartwig, *Am I a Redundant Human Being?*
John Hawkes, *The Passion Artist*
Dermot Healy, *Fighting with Shadows*
  *The Collected Short Stories*
Aidan Higgins, *A Bestiary*
  *Bornholm Night-Ferry*
  *Langrishe, Go Down*
  *Scenes from a Receding Past*
Aldous Huxley, *Point Counter Point*
  *Those Barren Leaves*
  *Time Must Have a Stop*
Drago Jančar, *The Galley Slave*
  *I Saw Her That Night*
  *The Tree with No Name*
Gert Jonke, *Awakening to the Great Sleep War*
  *Geometric Regional Novel*
  *Homage to Czerny*
  *The Distant Sound*
  *The System of Vienna*
Guillermo Cabrera Infante, *Infante's Inferno*
  *Three Trapped Tigers*
Jacques Jouet, *Mountain R*
Mieko Kanai, *The Word Book*
Yorum Kaniuk, *Life on Sandpaper*
Ignacy Karpowicz, *Gestures*
Pablo Katchadjian, *What to Do*
Hugh Kenner, *The Counterfeiters*
  *Flaubert, Joyce, and Beckett: The Stoic Comedian*
  *Gnomon*
  *Joyce's Voices*
Danilo Kiš, *A Tomb for Boris Davidovich*
  *Garden, Ashes*
Pierre Klossowski, *Roberte Ce Soir and The Revocation of the Edict of Nantes*
George Konrád, *The City Builder*
Tadeusz Konwicki, *The Polish Complex*
Elaine Kraf, *The Princess of 72nd Street*
Édouard Levé, *Suicide*
Mario Levi, *Istanbul Was a Fairytale*
Deborah Levy, *Billy & Girl*
José Lezama Lima, *Paradiso*
Osman Lins, *Avalovara*
António Lobo Antunes, *Knowledge of Hell*
  *The Splendor of Portugal*
Mina Loy, *Stories and Essays of Mina Loy*
Joaquim Maria Machado de Assis, *Collected Stories*
Alf Maclochlainn, *Out of Focus*
Ford Madox Ford, *The March of Literature*
D. Keith Mano, *Take Five*
Micheline Marcom, *A Brief History of Yes*
  *The Mirror in the Well*
Ben Marcus, *The Age of Wire and String*
Wallace Markfield, *Teitlebaum's Window*
  *To an Early Grave*
David Markson, *Reader's Block*
  *Wittgenstein's Mistress*
Carole Maso, *AVA*

**www.dalkeyarchive.com**

# www.dalkeyarchive.com

CPSIA information can be obtained
at www.ICGtesting.com
Printed in the USA
BVHW031322180119
538141BV00002B/4/P